Get **more** out of libraries

Please return or renew this item by the last date shown.

You can renew online at www.hants.gov.uk/library

Or by phoning 0845 603 5631

Hampshire
County Council

Sheriff Without a Star

Despite his four years of distinguished service Sheriff Cassidy Yates lost the confidence of Monotony's townsfolk because his error of judgement led to the death of Leland Matlock's son. But when the star Cassidy had worn with pride was removed from his chest, Leland claimed he knew something that would shed new light on the sheriff's downfall.

Before Leland could reveal what he knew he was shot, but Cassidy still had the instincts of a lawman. He believed Leland's shooting was connected to the death of his son and that if he could uncover the link it would restore the townsfolk's confidence in him. So Cassidy embarked on his greatest ever challenge: to get the star pinned back on his chest where it belonged.

Sheriff Without a Star

I.J. Parnham

A Black Horse Western

ROBERT HALE · LONDON

ISBN 978-0-7090-9232-2

Robert Hale Limited
Clerkenwell House
Clerkenwell Green
London EC1R 0HT

www.halebooks.com

Typeset by
Derek Doyle & Associates, Shaw Heath
Printed and bound in Great Britain by
CPI Antony Rowe, Chippenham and Eastbourne

PROLOGUE

'Do it tonight,' Henry Scott said, as he slapped the wad of bills into Rockwell Trent's hand. 'This late, Perry will be at home. He takes a stroll earlier in the evening, but—'

'Be quiet,' Rockwell snapped. He riffled through the bills, confirming the $200 he wanted was there. Then he lunged for Henry's collar and hoisted him up so that the two men could look at each other eye to eye. 'Do you know why they call me the Iceman?'

Henry flinched as Rockwell's knuckles brushed his chin.

'Your hands they're . . . they're frozen.'

Rockwell widened his eyes. 'They say ice runs in my veins. Some say I'm not even alive. Most don't dare say anything. So why is a miserable runt like you wasting my time by blabbering?'

'I-I wanted to be sure you'd complete the job.'

'I *always* complete the job.'

Rockwell threw Henry to the floor. On his side, Henry slid to a halt. Then, with a whimpered bleat, he rolled to his feet and scurried into hiding behind a table.

Rockwell uttered a snort of contempt. Then one steady pace at a time he backed away to the door. Still watching Henry, he opened the door. He glanced outside then sidled through the mercantile's doorway to stand on the boardwalk.

With sundown some hours past Carmon was bustling, but only around the saloon. This late, the torch brands that had been lit earlier in the evening were burning out.

Rockwell stood by the door, appraising the few people he saw. None of them was looking his way, but even so he ran his gaze to every person, across every window and along the tops of the false-fronted buildings before he strode into the road.

Perry Morgan's mercantile was on the opposite side of the road to Henry Scott's establishment. It was larger and the shining wares hanging in the polished windows suggested it was securing more trade than Henry's business was.

Rockwell headed for the alley beside the building and paced down it to the back. Earlier, he had wedged open the shutters to the downstairs window and so, after appraising the solitary light that was as usual illuminating the upstairs bedroom window, he slipped silently through the gap and into the back store.

6

For several minutes he stood, listening and letting his eyes become accustomed to the gloom. At first light he had paced out and memorized a route to the door that avoided any obstacles.

Sure enough, the outlines of the crates and boxes that filled the room in an untidy tangle were as he remembered them.

Although he'd practised the route with his eyes closed, Rockwell took several minutes to shuffle the ten yards to the door. He pushed the door open a fraction then edged through and stalked down the hall to the stairs.

He padded up the stairs, placing his feet on the edges of the wood to minimize creaking. Even so, he avoided the tenth stair, which always creaked.

At the top of the stairs, he slipped his six-shooter from its holster and held it beside his cheek aimed upwards. He didn't cock it. He paced to the door to Perry's bedroom. The light from within cast a rectangle of light around the door frame.

If Perry were facing him, when Rockwell opened the door he would be seen. But this late in the evening Perry enjoyed reading. With his poor eyesight, he would be hunched close to the light and have his back to the door.

Rockwell pushed the door, grabbing it before it could squeak, which it would do when it had swung open fully.

A large chair faced the lamp beside the window, its back to the door. An open book was on a side table. The lamp lit the pages that were rustling in the breeze from the doorway. As the chair was huge, it enveloped his quarry.

Rockwell edged inside and, leaving the door open, he paced across the room, placing his feet down with silent stealth.

As he closed on his target, he saw Perry's left hand draped over the side of the chair. The fingers were dangling and slack.

A puddle of blood was on the floor beneath that hand, the liquid inky and shining in the sallow lamplight. On the tip of Perry's index finger a drop of blood formed, bulged, then fell and plopped into the puddle, the sound echoing in the previously silent room.

Rockwell winced. In a swift movement he thrust his gun out. He covered the last three paces at speed and dragged the chair around.

Perry sat slumped, his mouth slack. An angry red hole in the centre of his forehead testified as to his fate. Slowly the body slid from the chair to lie on its back on the floor. Blank and unseeing eyes looked up at him.

Someone had already killed the man he had been hired to kill.

Rockwell ground his hand into a fist then slammed it against his hip as he peered through the window and into the darkness beyond.

'Not again,' he muttered.

CHAPTER 1

'Put your money away, Cassidy,' Jim Douglas said. 'You don't have to pay tonight.'

Sheriff Cassidy Yates raised his glass in silent salute, acknowledging the tribute the bartender had given him. In the four years he'd been coming into the Silver Streak, the best saloon in the township of Monotony, Jim had never once failed to charge him, no matter how much trouble he'd had to sort out.

'In that case,' Cassidy said, 'leave the bottle.'

Jim frowned but having made the offer he couldn't withdraw it. Cassidy smiled at his discomfort. Then, while nursing his glass against his chest, he leaned back against the bar and surveyed the teeming saloon room.

Perhaps in deference to tonight's importance, everyone was in good spirits and for once there was no sign of any trouble breaking out. So he topped up his glass, but he resolved that that would be his final drink tonight.

After all, for the next hour he was still on duty.

That duty weighed heavily when he saw who came into the saloon next. Leland Matlock pushed through the batwings and stomped to a halt a few paces in from the door. He picked out Cassidy and considered him with steely eyes that now complemented the steel colour of his receding hair.

Despite the passage of years one thing hadn't changed. Many of the customers tipped their hats to him, acknowledging his rare visit to the Silver Streak.

He murmured a few pleasantries as he walked across the room to stand at the bar. He chose a position ten feet from Cassidy, that being far enough away to avoid him, but close enough not to make it appear obvious that he was ignoring him.

The customers caught the significance of Cassidy and Leland being so close together for the first time in a year and silence reigned as they watched eagerly for developments. For most of that year they had studiously avoided each other, but since the elections when Edwin Johanson had been elected as the new sheriff Cassidy had seen more of Leland. It had always been at a distance, but he hadn't avoided looking at him.

A man with fewer principles than Leland Matlock might have behaved that way because he was gloating, but Cassidy reckoned he'd been moving towards accepting him. Although as it

10

turned out, Leland took his drink and stayed hunched over at the bar.

Presently, everybody returned to his business and the noise level rose to its former volume. So Cassidy put him from his mind and drank up his whiskey at a leisurely rate. When he'd finished, he pushed himself away from the bar and made his way past Leland towards the door.

'Cassidy,' Leland said when Cassidy was a few paces past him, his voice low and barely audible.

Although he had prepared himself for the possibility that Leland had come here this night of all nights specifically to see him, Cassidy still exhaled his breath loudly as he came to a halt.

He stayed looking at the door gathering his composure then turned to find Leland was still looking straight ahead. He joined him at the bar.

'Leland,' he said.

Leland poured him a drink, and even though Cassidy had resolved not to have another whiskey he moved for it, but when his fingers closed around the glass, Leland slapped a hand on his wrist. He nodded at the clock behind the bar.

'Not for another forty-five minutes,' he said.

Cassidy nodded and withdrew the hand.

'I understand,' he said.

'And then we can talk.' Leland leaned towards him. 'And not just about Walker. I need to tell you something, something that's too important for me to entrust it to Edwin Johanson.'

11

With that surprising revelation made the two men settled down to enjoy a surprisingly companionable silence similar to the ones they'd often enjoyed back in the days when their circumstances had been different.

Cassidy whiled away half of his remaining time as a lawman at the bar until there was just enough time to complete one last duty. He turned to the door.

'I'll be back soon for that drink and that chat,' he said.

'Your last patrol?' Leland asked.

'Yeah,' Cassidy said, finding that to his surprise his voice caught.

He coughed to cover his embarrassment and headed to the door. He'd reached it when a huge roar sounded behind him. He swirled round, expecting that trouble had broken out after all, but he found that every customer was looking at him.

Hats went flying up in the air and another roar sounded as everyone hurried over and surrounded him with a wall of good cheer. He looked over their heads to see that Leland wasn't watching the well-wishers then spread his hands and smiled.

His back resounded to numerous slaps and his hand was shaken so hard and so often it felt as if it might drop off. Everyone wished him well, even though many of them would have voted Edwin Johanson into office and some of them were people he'd slammed in jail before.

Cassidy enjoyed the unexpected attention. During his term as a lawman he had made one bad mistake and that had cost him his position, but it appeared that tonight all that was on everyone's minds were the hundreds of good decisions he'd made.

By the time he'd extricated himself from the well-wishers and slipped outside, the clock on the Shaw Hotel wall opposite the saloon said it was eight minutes to midnight.

He stood on the boardwalk with the customers grinning at him over the top of the batwings and his ears ringing with their support. He sighed, accepting he no longer had enough time to patrol around town for one last time.

He tipped his hat to the customers, received a last cheer, then with a smile on his lips he walked down the road towards the law office. Even if he couldn't patrol, he could do the only other thing he'd decided he would do tonight.

He stopped in the doorway to the law office and with his arms folded, as he had often done in quiet moments late at night, he watched the clock hands circle round.

He resolved that when the minute hand clicked round to the upright position he would go inside and place his star on his desk. After that he would go back to the Silver Streak and have that drink with Leland, and perhaps reconcile the one failing in his term as a lawman in Monotony.

Five minutes remained when Deputy Floyd Wright came outside to join him.

'Quiet night,' he said in a matter-of-fact manner, as if this was any other night.

'Enjoy them when you can,' Cassidy said.

'I intend to. If they continue, you deserve the credit.'

'And you. You've been a good deputy. Johanson won't go wrong with you to guide him.'

Floyd frowned. 'I don't know what his plans for me are. I haven't spoken to him since he was—'

A distant gunshot sounded, the rattle echoing in the road, but seemingly coming from outside the Shaw Hotel.

The few people that were on the boardwalks were in patches of light, and they all looked around while cringing away towards the nearest walls. Cassidy beckoned to Floyd as he set off.

'Come on,' he said.

'You can't—' Floyd began, but he silenced when Cassidy shot him a harsh glare.

'I'm still the sheriff,' Cassidy said. 'I'll sort this out.'

Floyd nodded. 'Then hurry. In four minutes this is Edwin Johanson's problem.'

Cassidy returned the nod then looked ahead for movement. The gunshot had caught the attention of the customers in the Silver Streak. People were craning their necks over the batwings and they were all looking to the Shaw Hotel.

With few lights being on in the rooms, the hotel was a forbidding and silent block in the night. Alleys were on either side of the building. When Cassidy looked down the left-hand one he didn't see anyone there.

So he directed Floyd to head down that alley and explore behind the hotel while he took the right-hand alley.

He glanced at the clock, noting that it was three minutes to midnight. With his gun drawn he stood beside the alley and listened for any noises coming from within.

With a rueful smile he decided that this was a better way to end his time as sheriff rather than merely waiting outside until midnight. He slipped around the corner, keeping his back to the wall to limit his profile.

A hulking shape was ten feet away, the large form silhouetted against the slither of sky at the other end of the alley and catching some light filtering in from the road.

Cassidy edged sideways towards the form, unable to make out what he was seeing. It was too large to be a man, but he could see no other explanation for the obstruction.

The form moved and he caught a glimpse of eyes staring at him in the gloom. Lower down another glint caught a stray beam of light, this time of gunmetal.

15

Cassidy swung his gun around a moment before an explosion of gunfire tore out. The slug was ill-directed and clattered into the wall to his right before careening out into the road towards the saloon. Cassidy still ducked away. When he heard receding footfalls he jerked back up.

Cassidy loosed off a warning shot at the fleeing man, but within moments the man reached the safety of the end of the alley and disappeared from view. Cassidy set off after him, but he slid to a halt when he saw that another dark form was still ahead on the ground.

He moved to the side to improve the available light and saw that a body was lying before him. He went to one knee and identified the body as being Leland Matlock's, the man he'd been speaking to in the saloon only fifteen minutes ago.

It was too dark to be sure of his condition, but he consoled himself with the observation that Leland was well enough to murmur in pain. Cassidy patted his shoulder then hurried on down the alley after the shooter.

He paused at the end then ducked down to come out with his body doubled-over. He was pleased he'd been cautious when a gunshot pinged off the corner of the wall above his head.

Cassidy threw himself to the ground as another slug whined past him. He landed with his arms thrust straight out and with his elbows planted to the ground to hold his gun firm.

16

The shooter was twenty yards ahead, running sideways along the back of the Shaw Hotel, his ambling gait letting him look both ahead and back to Cassidy.

'Halt!' Cassidy cried as he got the man in his sights.

The man did just that, but he also swung his gun round. Cassidy tightened his trigger-finger, but before he could fire Deputy Wright leapt in a blur of motion out of the other alley. He caught the man around the stomach with his outstretched arms and carried him on for several paces until both men went tumbling to the ground.

Floyd landed on top and tried to pin his quarry down, but the man bucked him. They rolled to the side.

As both men struggled to get the upper hand Cassidy jumped to his feet and broke into a run. He kept his gun trained on the fighting twosome, but in the poor light and with the men being entangled he didn't risk shooting.

He was halfway towards them when Floyd's assailant tore himself away from the deputy's grasp. He slapped a palm under Floyd's chin, pushing him on to his back, before moving to a kneeling position.

He jerked his gun up to aim at Floyd, but he didn't get to fire when Cassidy pounded over the last few yards and kicked the weapon from his grasp.

17

The man went down clutching his hand and when he looked up, he was staring down the barrel of Cassidy's gun.

'You,' Cassidy said, 'are under arrest.'

As the man glared up at him, Floyd spoke up from the ground.

'You can't say that,' he said.

'Why not? I—'

Cassidy sighed. The heat of the chase had made him forget about the time. It would now be past midnight and so, for the first time in four years, he was no longer a lawman.

He took a backward pace to let Floyd take over.

'Now you,' Floyd said, getting to his feet, 'are under arrest.'

18

CHAPTER 2

'Why are you here, Cassidy?' Sheriff Edwin Johanson asked. 'You *have* remembered you're not the sheriff no more, haven't you?'

Cassidy forced a laugh. 'I had remembered, but I thought you'd want to question me about what happened last night.'

Johanson shrugged, his pout suggesting this was the last thing on his mind.

'No. If I need your help, I'll find you.'

Johanson gave Cassidy a curt nod. Then, with a determined swing of the head, he looked down at the sheet of paper on his desk.

With the new sheriff making it obvious that he didn't want to talk with the old sheriff, Cassidy looked around the law office. It was only mid-morning on Johanson's first day, but the clutter had already been tidied away.

Deputy Wright wasn't here, although from the adjoining jailhouse the sounds of vigorous scrubbing could be heard.

Cassidy rocked from foot to foot, for the first time feeling uncertain in what had been his domain. He backed away for a pace then moved towards the door, but with Johanson studiously ignoring him he felt he couldn't slink out in this way.

'You need to make this job your own,' he said, 'but I can help you. And not just with dealing with that man last night.'

Johanson stayed looking at his sheet of paper for longer than was polite then slowly looked up at him.

'I know you have a personal interest in Leland Matlock's affairs, so you can rest assured that I'll find the man who shot him.'

Cassidy narrowed his eyes. 'But we caught him. There's no finding to be done.'

'That'll be the difference between your term as sheriff and mine, and why I won't seek out your help. I don't jump to conclusions like you did. The prisoner – Zachary McKinney – will be released when I've checked out his story.'

'Released?' Cassidy spluttered. 'Floyd and I saw him shoot Leland.'

'Neither of you saw Zachary shoot anyone. You heard a gunshot and came across him kneeling beside Leland. Zachary set off to find the man who'd shot him, but with you giving chase and shooting wildly he thought you were Leland's

20

assailant and defended himself. It's likely your intervention only succeeded in stopping him catching the real culprit.'

Cassidy explored Johanson's eyes, wondering if he'd been joking, but when he met his gaze, he took a deep breath before he replied.

'In my time here I've heard some tall tales. That one's more brazen than most.'

'And one you'd reject?'

'I sure would.'

'Then I'm glad your term ended last night. Millicent Matlock hired Zachary to ensure Leland came to no harm. Zachary failed in that duty, but he wouldn't kill the man he'd been hired to protect.'

Cassidy shrugged. 'I didn't know that, but for a man who doesn't jump to conclusions, I'm surprised you've already concluded Zachary wouldn't kill Leland.'

Johanson sneered. 'I don't care how surprised you are because this doesn't concern an *ex*-lawman.'

Johanson looked down at his desk and this time Cassidy backed away and opened the door. But he stopped in the doorway and watched Johanson move paper around.

The new sheriff was right. He shouldn't have offered uninvited opinions when his only role was as a witness, but that didn't stop him being irritated.

Being voted out of office had been bad enough, but being treated with offhand contempt afterwards only went to worsen the insult. For the last few weeks he had been resigned to his fate, but now that he no longer wore the star, from deep in his chest a nugget of anger grew.

He gripped his hands tightly to fight down the rage and slowly a new thought formed that made him smile.

'Johanson,' he said, 'remember this: I won't be an ex-lawman forever, but one day soon you will be. So keep my star clean for me.'

Before Johanson could retort he turned away then walked down the road, enjoying the new sense of purpose he'd gathered.

With his intentions now made clear to Johanson that somehow he would once again be sheriff, he thought back to last night. Before he'd been shot Leland Matlock had appeared ready to seek reconciliation with him, and he'd claimed to have something important to tell him.

With Leland being seriously hurt, he probably wasn't accepting visitors, but even so for the first time in a year Cassidy headed to his house.

It was a large building on the edge of town, and after he'd knocked at the door Doc Taylor appeared.

'If you've come to pay your last respects,' the doctor said, his eyebrows shooting up in surprise, 'you're too early, I hope.'

'I hope so too,' Cassidy said. 'But does that mean it's looking bad?'

'I don't have to discuss that with you no more.' Taylor shrugged. 'But he's an old man and the next few days will be crucial.'

'I'd still like to see him.'

'You can, but whether he sees you is another matter. He's asleep and probably will be for a while.' Taylor bit his lip, appearing to consider whether he should mention something, then gave a slight shrug. 'Millicent is with him.'

Cassidy winced. When he'd decided to visit he'd not considered that she'd be caring for her father-in-law. But then again, if he'd come here to heal one wound, maybe she was another wound he should try to heal.

'I'd like to see them both,' he said.

Taylor blew out his cheeks, his wide eyes registering surprise.

'Then that's even more of a damn fool notion.'

Despite his comment Taylor stepped back from the door letting Cassidy enter. He pointed to the last door in the long hall, a room that had been a study when Leland had been a close confidant. They had often sat in that study and discussed town matters.

They would never do that again, but even if he were unlikely to get a response from Leland, it would probably be preferable to the reaction he'd get from Millicent.

Sure enough, before he'd reached the door, Millicent poked her head out into the hall to see who was coming. She flinched back in surprise, her open-mouthed expression registering a mixture of horror and another strong emotion, perhaps disgust.

She gathered her composure and raised a hand to halt him. While holding on to the door jamb she darted back into the room, presumably checking that Leland could be left alone, then closed the door almost to and joined him.

She began to say something, her lips thin and disapproving, then changed her mind and set off down the hall, heading for the lounge into which Doc Taylor had retired.

'Why did you let *him* in?' she asked as she went through the door.

'I thought he had a right,' Taylor said as Cassidy followed her through, 'to make his peace with—'

She slammed her hands on her hips. 'He's the last person Leland would want to see.'

'Perhaps, but—' Taylor looked away. Embarrassment coloured his cheeks, perhaps because he'd thought of saying that Cassidy had also come to see her, or perhaps from thinking that Leland wasn't in a position to say who saw him.

'I don't want to hear excuses,' she said. 'Show him out and don't let him in again, even after Leland gets better.'

She turned to the door, swirling her skirt, and

24

moved to walk past Cassidy without looking at him.

'I'm sorry this happened,' Cassidy said.

His comment halted her in her tracks. She bunched her jaw as she stared straight ahead while struggling to find the words to reply.

'You're not sorry,' she said, turning to him, her eyes blank reflective surfaces. 'Aside from whoever shot him, you're the only one who's enjoying this. But you won't get a chance to gloat because he will live and he will recover.'

'I hope he does.'

'Why?'

'If only to prove you wrong. I don't like the thought of you having such a low opinion of me.'

'And why would you care about my feelings? What we had died two years ago.'

Having now succeeded in getting her talking, Cassidy found that their conversation had taken an uncomfortable direction. He passed over the many things he wanted to say and settled for stating a simple truth.

'I don't bear Leland ill will because of what happened at Riker's Bend and the same goes for you.'

She snorted. 'Then I'll tell you something. He bears you nothing but ill will. And so do I!'

Her eyes blazed, defying him to retort. He knew that before she walked away he had only seconds to ask one of the many questions he wanted to ask, so he settled for the direct approach.

'Last night Leland spoke to me in the Silver

Streak. He wanted to tell me something, but he got shot before we could speak about it. Maybe it concerned the reason you hired Zachary McKinney to protect him?'

Anger narrowed her eyes. 'You're not the sheriff no more. Questions like that are no concern of yours.'

She gathered her wits and did the one thing he'd expected her to do for the last year. She delivered a stinging slap to his cheek that rocked his head to the side.

While Cassidy rubbed his burning cheek she stormed away and slammed the door shut behind her. Cassidy listened to her heels clicking down the hall. Taylor joined him.

'Why did you really come?' he asked, his voice soft.

'For the reason I said,' Cassidy said. 'I reckon Leland was ready to forgive me.'

Taylor shrugged. 'As with Millicent I can't see him doing that this side of the Pearly Gates. I'd guess that he wanted to speak to you about Benjamin Shaw. I've heard he's likely to get a pardon.'

Cassidy winced. 'I didn't know that. But you have to be wrong. They'd never let that killer walk free.'

'Cassidy, I'm telling you this because I trust you. You were the only one who saw what happened at Riker's Bend. Some think that a man who made so many other mistakes that night might also have been wrong about Benjamin.'

'I know what I saw,' Cassidy said for not the first time in the last year. Then he too stormed out the room slamming the door behind him.

In the Hunter's Moon Saloon in Bear Creek, Rockwell Trent hunched over his third whiskey.

Usually when the Iceman drank in a saloon, he sat at a table by the wall where he could face the door. There, he could watch everyone in the saloon and anyone who entered or left. If someone made the mistake of coming near him, one flash of his cold eyes would force them to drink elsewhere.

But tonight his brooding irritation had led him to stand at the bar where he paid only minimal attention to the cowboys milling around. Although, as usual, he'd generated a zone of space around him that nobody ventured within.

No matter how much he pondered, his mood didn't lighten.

Twice in the last month Rockwell had found the person he'd been hired to kill already dead. Once wasn't strange as the people he killed usually had enemies aplenty, but twice in succession was unusual, and the manner of their deaths, shot between the eyes, matched Rockwell's trademark method of dispatch.

This might have been a coincidence, but even if it was Rockwell hated the unexpected.

27

With a short gesture he knocked back his drink, but as he reached for the whiskey bottle, from the corner of his eye he glimpsed a man looking sideways at him from further down the bar.

Rockwell still poured himself a short measure. He sipped it, but stood tall, using the mirror behind the bar to look around the saloon.

The man now had his head down, his hat hiding his face, and everybody else he could see was engaged in his own conversation and not looking his way.

Still, Rockwell pushed himself from the bar. He threw a dollar on the counter and paced towards the door. As he pulled his hat low, he flicked a glance at the man who had looked his way, but this man kept his back to him.

On the boardwalk, Rockwell looked up and down the road. Nobody was looking at him and nobody was making an obvious display of avoiding noticing him. He headed down the boardwalk past his horse and continued until he reached the alley beside the saloon.

There, he slipped to the side disappearing into the alley's shadows and pressed his back to the saloon wall.

He waited and within a minute, as he'd expected, the man who had looked at him wandered past the alley, his head darting in all directions as he searched up and down the road.

The man was stocky and he wasn't packing a gun

28

but, even so, Rockwell slipped out of the alley and followed him. He placed his feet to the boardwalk with deliberate care, limiting any sound.

They passed a mercantile and a barber's shop. Outside each, the man glanced through the windows and into the darkened interiors, displaying obvious signs of looking for him.

Few people were outside and nobody was walking on this side of the road, so ten yards away from the next alley, Rockwell hurried to a trot.

His sudden patter of footfalls alerted his quarry and he swung round, but by then, Rockwell was on him and had pressed a firm hand over his mouth.

He pulled him back to his chest and walked him into the alley. There, he slammed the barrel of his gun against the man's temple, grinding the cold metal in.

'You're following me,' he muttered.

A muffled grunt sounded against Rockwell's hand.

'I'll take that for a yes,' Rockwell said.

He drew the hand from his face then swung the man away, making him hit the opposite wall before he rebounded for a pace and straightened up. His eyes rolled in to focus on the gun aimed at his forehead.

'You can,' the man murmured, his voice shaking. He tore his gaze from the gun to look at Rockwell. 'I hope you remember me.'

Rockwell appraised him then nodded.

'It's been a while.' Rockwell still kept his gun aimed at the man's head.

'It has.' The man shrugged his jacket and stood as tall as his short frame would allow. 'Yet the Iceman is still as sharp as he ever was.'

'Quit the fancy talk.'

'Then I'll get to the point. I want to hire you again.'

Rockwell narrowed his eyes. 'It didn't go so well for you the last time.'

'That'll make revenge all the sweeter.'

'I don't think like other men. I still operate in the same way. Pay in advance or my gun stays holstered.' With a twirl of his wrist Rockwell slipped his gun into its holster.

The man blew out his cheeks. 'This time, I'm not prepared to pay in advance.'

'Then you'll leave the alley first. Don't follow me.'

The man winked and raised a hand. 'Don't be hasty. I'm not prepared to pay in advance because this time I'll pay ten times your usual rate.'

Rockwell licked his lips. 'Then you just got my undivided attention.'

CHAPTER 3

As Cassidy made his way down the road he saw that while he'd been in Leland's house around a dozen people had gathered ahead. Closer to the group he saw they were congregating outside Stanley Shaw's hotel. Sheriff Johanson was amongst them, gesturing for everyone to leave.

Cassidy didn't want Johanson to see him coming from the direction of Leland's house and so he slipped into the Silver Streak. He purchased a whiskey then hunched over at the bar pondering.

He considered the brief conversation he'd had with Leland last night, but he couldn't tease out any additional details that would let him work out what he had wanted to tell him. Millicent hadn't refuted Johanson's claim that she'd hired Zachary McKinney to protect Leland, and even if she hadn't given him her reason, it was clear she must have feared for his life.

The question then was who would have tried to

31

kill him, but no matter how long he brooded over the circumstances no name would come to mind. . . .

'Cassidy Yates,' someone said beside him, interrupting his thoughts. 'As in no longer *Sheriff* Cassidy Yates.'

Cassidy turned to find he was facing Dodge Elwood. The old troublemaker was smirking, his rolling eyes and wild hair bristling with barely suppressed glee.

'Should have realized it was you,' Cassidy sniffed, silently conveying his insult. 'If there's one thing I won't miss about being a lawman, it'll be dealing with men like you.'

Dodge snorted a mocking burst of laughter, although his narrowed eyes showed he wasn't amused. He produced a sheet of paper from behind his back. A genuine smile appeared as he waved it at him.

'You seen this?'

Cassidy glanced at the paper, noting the columns of scrawled handwriting.

'Why? Do you want me to read it to you?'

'Nope. I thought you'd like to sign it.' Dodge looked over his shoulder at the bulk of the saloon's customers and grinned. He received grunts of encouragement.

'What is it?' Cassidy asked, seeing no way to avoid stepping into whatever trap Dodge has set for him.

'It's a pet . . . petty . . . petition,' Dodge said, his struggle to pronounce suggesting he had never uttered the word before. He placed the paper before his face and moved his eyes from side to side, pretending to read the text. 'We the under-signed wish to state as a matter of record that we believe Benjamin Shaw has been the victim of a—'

Cassidy snatched the paper from Dodge's grasp and swirled it round to continue reading. Dodge was right. It was a petition to be sent to the state governor asking for a pardon for Benjamin Shaw.

Numerous signatures were below the opening statement. In Cassidy's brief scan he noted the names of several people who he'd have thought would never sign such a petition.

Having confirmed what the paper was, he started reading from the top, reading each name and looking for certain people, but then he real-ized that Dodge had goaded him into providing the reaction he'd wanted. He slapped the paper against Dodge's chest and turned back to the bar.

'Go away,' he grunted.

'I'm not. I reckon the whole town will sign it, so you should too if you know what's good for you. It's the—'

'Leave! I'm not signing no petition.'

Cassidy knew he shouldn't let Dodge annoy him, but the petition was the worst betrayal he'd had so far. He bunched his fists to fight down an urge to tear it from Dodge's grasp and rip it into pieces.

'The day's passed,' Dodge said, 'when you could talk to me like that. Show respect, *Mister* Yates.'

Dodge waved the petition in Cassidy's face and this time Cassidy let his anger get the better of him. He shoved Dodge away. It was only a light push but Dodge still stumbled and he had to grab hold of the bar to stop himself falling.

An aggrieved groan went up from the customers and chairs scraped back as those people stood. Dodge had exaggerated the strength of the push to gain sympathy, but the angle at which he'd been standing would have masked what had happened and made Cassidy's minor action appear worse than it had been.

Dodge grinned as he righted himself. He placed the petition on the bar then raised his fists and advanced on Cassidy as he prepared to pay him back for the many times Cassidy had thrown him in a cell. Cassidy stood his ground, waiting for Dodge to make the mistake of throwing the first punch.

'Cassidy!' the familiar voice of Deputy Wright shouted from behind him. 'Leave Dodge alone.'

Dodge halted his advance and glanced over Cassidy's shoulder.

'Go away,' he grunted.

'Quit complaining. I'm helping you.' Floyd paced across the saloon to stand beside Cassidy. 'I don't want you getting beaten to a pulp.'

Dodge grumbled, but with Floyd glaring at him

and giving him no option, he turned away. The customers who'd stood to watch the confrontation sat down and with the situation ending before it'd taken a turn for the worse, Cassidy accepted Floyd's invitation to leave.

'Obliged for your help,' he said when they were outside and walking down the boardwalk towards the hotel. People were still milling around, but Sheriff Johanson wasn't amongst them. 'But I could have dealt with Dodge Elwood.'

'I know, but it's my duty to keep the peace. That means I stop saloon brawls before they break out.'

This reminder of their new roles made Cassidy wince. He'd not been a lawman for less than a day and already he'd made the mistake of forgetting his current status. He stopped and spread his hands as he offered an apology.

'Sorry I nearly got into a fight, but it wasn't my doing.'

'I know. That's why I came. I knew about the petition.' Floyd provided an apologetic smile. 'And judging by your calm expression you didn't notice, so you should hear it from me first: my name's on it.'

Floyd's was one of the names he'd been looking for and the news did hurt him.

'It must be hard for you now,' Cassidy said after a moment's thought. 'I saw Edwin Johanson's name and you have to make sure you keep your job.'

Floyd acknowledged Cassidy's explanation with

a relieved smile. Cassidy didn't know if that was the reason why he'd signed, but he could live with it.

'We need to put the past behind us and make a fresh start.' Floyd considered Cassidy. 'So is that why you went to see Leland Matlock?'

'Sure,' Cassidy said with a smile, noting that even if Johanson hadn't seen him, his eagle-eyed deputy had.

'Don't lie to me, Cassidy. Johanson told me you want to be sheriff again. That'll never happen, so if you've learnt anything, tell me and I'll deal with it.'

'Obliged for the speech, Deputy Wright. You're getting better at it all the time.' Cassidy raised his eyebrows and widened his smile. 'Now tell me everything you know about Leland and Zachary McKinney.'

For several seconds Floyd kept his jaw set firm and Cassidy wondered if he would decline the opportunity to lighten his mood. Finally, Floyd returned the smile. He glanced around to check that nobody was within earshot, but he still drew Cassidy closer to the wall.

'This will surprise you,' he said, 'but I reckon Johanson's right. Millicent hired Zachary because she was worried Benjamin Shaw would be released soon. She paid him well, so Zachary wouldn't end their arrangement.'

Cassidy leaned forward to look into Floyd's eyes.

'You've spent too much time with Johanson

36

already. You're getting lazy. He's a good enough lawman to uncover the facts, but you used to be good enough to uncover the truth.' Cassidy widened his eyes. 'What's the one aspect of that story that's still unknown?'

'Why did a man who was paid as well as Zachary was let Leland wander off on his own down a dark alley?' Floyd replied.

'There's hope for you yet.' Cassidy straightened and waggled a finger at Floyd. 'Keep that inquisitive nature and don't let Johanson grind it out of you.'

'I won't, but—' Floyd frowned, as if he was considering whether to mention something, then shrugged. 'But in truth something else happened last night that's been taking up our time. A woman was murdered in the Shaw Hotel; shot between the eyes.'

'Connected?'

Floyd chuckled. 'You sure do miss the work. But I don't know. We don't even know for sure who she was yet. She'd just arrived in town. She was old, but she was painted up, so she might have been planning to set up a business in competition with Rosie. Johanson's questioning her.'

'Shooting doesn't sound like Rosie's style.'

'Perhaps not, but whoever killed her stole her belongings and searching Rosie's place for them is a good way to start the investigation.'

Cassidy nodded. When he'd been sheriff,

raiding the Pink Lady had always been a good way of solving crimes, and not necessarily the ones he had been investigating.

'Then I wish you luck. I'll keep you informed if I learn anything.'

Floyd shook his head. 'You won't because you'll learn nothing to keep me informed about. I know this is hard for you, what with the matter of Walker Matlock still dragging on, but it's too late to put that right now. Move on and forget about this.'

'I made Johanson a promise. I'll make you the same one.' Cassidy slapped his hands on his hips. 'I will get my star back.'

Floyd considered him then relaxed the tense set of his shoulders.

'I hope you do. Johanson's a desk-bound politician, not a lawman.'

'So will you help me?'

Floyd looked around to check that nobody was close. He gave a brief nod before he left him to return to the sheriff's office.

Cassidy stood on the boardwalk for a while considering. Then he headed down the road to the hotel.

When he arrived, people were still milling around outside gossiping. This time he used more subtlety than he'd shown with Millicent and merged in with the group. He encouraged the gossip and confirmed the facts he'd been told, along with a few snippets of information Floyd hadn't divulged.

The woman had arrived last night by train. She'd not spoken to anyone and had gone straight to her hotel room. In the early hours of the morning she'd been shot with a single bullet to the forehead. She had fallen beside the door, presumably after having opened it. Although nobody knew where she'd come from, they did know she'd booked into the hotel under the name of Elizabeth Caine.

Despite the lateness of the hour she had been dressed, implying she had been expecting her visitor. When the gossips began adding in clearly fabricated lurid details, he left them then headed into the alley where last night he'd come across Zachary McKinney hunched over Leland Matlock.

When he'd been a lawman, he'd always tried to see the situation from the victim's viewpoint, so he peered down the alley, as Leland would have done before the incident.

This didn't bring any new thoughts to mind and so Cassidy turned away. But as he left the alley, he looked down and there, fluttering in the breeze and caught beneath a stone was a scrap of paper.

Cassidy picked it up, confirming it was just a slither of paper, but with his eyes now attuned to what he should be looking for he saw other pieces.

For the next ten minutes he crawled around gathering up a dozen of these scraps. They were broadly of the same size. Several had writing on them, although none was big enough for him to make out even a single word. But he found enough to add to the theory he had already formulated that Elizabeth's murder was connected to the attack on Leland.

He reckoned Elizabeth had come to town to see Leland. She had sent him a message and despite the presence of his hired gun this had worried Leland. So he had gone to the saloon, perhaps to see him or perhaps just to ponder on whether he should see her. While the customers were applauding Cassidy, he had gone to the hotel where he'd loitered outside while tearing up her message. He'd been shot before he'd made up his mind and his shooter had then gone on to kill her.

When Cassidy had learnt everything he could from the scene of the shooting, he rode out of town. At a hurried pace he headed back to his house where he gathered enough belongings for a few days' travel.

In the early afternoon, less than a day after he was no longer officially allowed to investigate Leland Matlock's assault, he rode away from town. He went westwards along the rail tracks ready to start an investigation that he hoped would help him reclaim the star that was rightly his.

CHAPTER 4

As Cassidy rode on towards Destitution, the nearest westward town, he dwelt on the reasons why he was so determined to reclaim his star.

It had been four years since he had ridden into Monotony, found it a pleasant place, and decided to stay.

Fifteen years earlier Leland Matlock had founded the town. The tale of that founding had passed into legend. Leaving a Texas-bound wagon train with a baby courtesy of a tragedy en route that had taken the young mother, Leland had taken over an ailing trading post. Years of dedication had created a town and a seemingly unstoppable man, until now.

Leland's wounding saddened Cassidy more than he cared to admit. But his instincts told him that he would find Elizabeth's murderer and work out why Leland had been attacked only after he'd found out where she had come from, who she was,

41

and why she'd come to town.

His instincts also told him that resolving this matter would put right the reason why he'd lost his star in the first place.

So at a mile-eating pace he rode on, but with the nearest town still over thirty miles away, that night he settled down beside a stream.

With a fire roaring and his belly full, he considered, as he often did, the events of last year that had led to the current situation.

His only uttered comment was the one that had sustained him during the difficult times that had followed.

'I know what I saw.'

It had been a balmy summer night and Cassidy had been in the Silver Streak enjoying the evening with Deputy Wright. . . .

'You lousy varmint,' Walker Matlock shouted in the bustling saloon room behind him. 'Take that back.'

'I sure won't!' Benjamin Shaw retorted.

Cassidy turned from the bar to see that the two young men were standing in the middle of the saloon room confronting each other. The customers were displaying the usual mixture of reactions with some urging them to calm down and others goading them on to do the opposite.

'You going to step in?' Floyd asked, eyeing the developing confrontation.

'Nope,' Cassidy said. 'Benjamin's level-headed.'

'He is, but he's not the one I'm worried about.'

Cassidy nodded. Walker was a troublemaker, but his father always excused his only son's actions as being youthful exuberance, so Cassidy's attempts to stamp down his authority had fallen on deaf ears.

On the other hand, Benjamin was a polite young man who'd never given Cassidy cause to speak to him in an official capacity. In fact Cassidy reckoned he'd follow his father into becoming a respected businessman and perhaps even the town mayor one day.

'Stepping in too early,' Cassidy said, 'lets the resentment fester on and that causes even worse trouble later.'

Floyd raised his eyebrows in surprise but he said nothing as Benjamin shouted with uncharacteristic anger.

'Stay away from her!'

Walker looked Benjamin up and down, sneering with the arrogance of a man who thought he could best his opponent.

'Can't do that. She's bored with playing with boys and now she wants a man.'

This comment made Cassidy wince as he could guess which woman they were arguing over, but it made Benjamin react in an even worse manner. His eyes flared as he snorted his breath through his nostrils. Then he struck out.

43

Walker probably hadn't expected the normally placid young man to get so annoyed as to hit him or to have used such ferocity, so the sharp uppercut to his chin stood him straight. He lost his balance and wheeled backwards into the people standing behind him, felling three men before he tumbled to the floor.

An appreciative round of derision and encouragement sounded.

The felled men extricated themselves with much pushing and grumbling, adding to the onlookers' merriment. So by the time Walker got to his feet, embarrassment reddened his face.

Cassidy left the bar, preparing to step in when he needed to. He watched Walker finger his jaw, taking his time, then pace towards Benjamin.

The hooting silenced, but Benjamin kept his fists down, appearing as if he'd worked off his anger.

This didn't deter Walker. He waded in and delivered a swinging haymaker of a punch that would have thrown Benjamin clear across the room – if it had connected. But Benjamin ducked under it and came up with a calm expression on his face that only went to annoy Walker even more.

Walker grunted an oath then tried to deliver a short-armed jab to Benjamin's stomach, but Benjamin danced back on his toes, again avoiding the blow. So Walker let his momentum carry him on and threw out his arms, aiming to gather

Benjamin up in a bear hug.

This time his arms brushed Benjamin's chest, but Benjamin dropped to his knees so that Walker's arms closed on air. Benjamin drove up, slamming his shoulders into Walker's stomach and lifting him off the floor.

Then Benjamin stood with the bulky Walker suspended in the air, but when the weight made his knees buckle he moved to a table and tossed him from his shoulders.

Walker did a half-somersault before he landed on his back on the table, which collapsed under his weight, making him crash to the floor within a jumble of splinters and broken wood.

As catcalling resounded around the saloon, Benjamin took a deep breath and turned to the bar, his expression still calm as if his success had taken no effort and brought him no joy.

With the space that had opened up for the fight filling with customers, Cassidy looked at the wrecked table. The groggy Walker had stood and was batting the debris from his clothes. His posture didn't appear defeated as his gaze bored into Benjamin's back with obvious intent.

Cassidy headed towards him. His often-uttered speech about not taking the matter any further was on his lips, but then died.

Walker rolled his shoulders. A hand slipped inside his jacket, his gaze intent on Benjamin as he waited for his opponent to stand in clear space.

45

He didn't complete his planned action.

A gunshot rang out clipping the butt of the emerging gun and making Walker screech then flinch his hand away. As the gun slipped back into his jacket, he thrust his hand up to his face to examine the bloodied fingers.

'Relax,' Cassidy said in the suddenly quiet saloon. 'I've not shot off your fingers – yet.'

Walker's eyes blazed as if he might risk going for his gun despite the fact that Cassidy's drawn gun said he wouldn't finish that move. So Cassidy went over to him, opened his jacket, and removed the concealed weapon. Walker sneered, but then he looked to the door and his anger faded away.

From the corner of his eye Cassidy saw Leland Matlock step inside.

'What happened?' Leland said with his usual quiet dignity.

Although Walker had now relaxed his stance and folded his arms, Cassidy walked sideways, keeping him in view as he approached Leland.

'Your son was about to be foolish,' he said. 'I stopped him.'

Walker put on a shame-faced look as he examined his bloodied fingers.

'I weren't, Pa,' he bleated with exaggerated hurt feelings. 'The sheriff hates me. And we know why.'

Leland took in the situation. He considered Cassidy's drawn gun, the broken table, Benjamin's red face, his son's dishevelled state.

46

'Anybody other than Cassidy see my son go for a gun?' he asked. He listened to the murmured denials then turned to Cassidy. 'Then you must lock up Benjamin Shaw.'

'If I lock up anyone, it'll be Walker,' Cassidy said. 'He was set on killing Benjamin.'

Leland didn't reply immediately. He walked past Benjamin, looking him up and down, then joined his son. He turned to Cassidy.

'So you claim that Benjamin, a man without a bruise on him is the victim, and my son who's covered in dust, has a bruised jaw and blood on his fingers is the aggressor?'

If Cassidy were to detail the events, it'd confirm that Walker had goaded Benjamin on until he hit him, but he didn't want to embarrass anyone. He was searching for the right words to end the situation amicably when Benjamin spoke up.

'Leland's right,' he said. 'I started the fight. I ended it. If the sheriff arrests anyone, it should be me.'

Triumph flashed in Leland's eyes, but then Walker spoke up.

'Yeah,' he muttered with bad grace. 'Lock the dog up and let him rot.'

Leland may have indulged his wayward son, but he shot him a cold glare that silenced him then nodded towards the door, ordering him to leave.

Without another word Walker did as ordered, although he took a route that unnecessarily passed

47

by Benjamin and included a glare and a break in stride. Leland came over to Cassidy.

'Obliged if you'd deal with this,' he said, keeping his voice low. 'Lock Benjamin up until he's calmed down.'

'And Walker?'

Leland hunched his shoulders, his jaw grinding as if his answer took a lot of effort before he whispered the words that Cassidy had wanted to hear for the last few months.

'I'll deal with him. This ends here.'

When Leland had followed his son out of the saloon, Benjamin turned to Cassidy and put his hands together with a resigned gesture of accepting he would be clapped in handcuffs.

Even without Leland's intervention Cassidy had intended to take Benjamin aside and tell him his behaviour had been unacceptable. But Benjamin's lack of triumph and his acceptance of his punishment convinced him that he should be lenient.

Still, Cassidy walked towards him with his expression stern. Benjamin gulped, but Cassidy shepherded him away and led him to the bar.

'What was the problem?' Cassidy asked as the customers returned to enjoying their night's entertainment.

'A woman,' Benjamin murmured, providing a shamefaced look.

'Millicent's pretty, but she's married now. You shouldn't be—'

48

'Not her. It's Jane Thompson from the Bar W ranch.' Benjamin waited for a response but as Cassidy could think of nothing to say he continued, 'Walker's not content with being wed to a good woman; he was sniffing around mine, just because Leland's son can get away with anything.'

Cassidy bit back his irritation. Last year he'd lost out to the younger Walker in the attempt to win the heart of Millicent Graham and if Walker was now likely to distress her, that doubly hurt him.

'Some might say that being the son of the mayor of Monotony lets you take liberties too.'

'I've never done nothing. . . .' Benjamin winced as he clearly recalled the events of the last ten minutes. 'It won't happen again, Sheriff.'

'But that'll be hard.' Cassidy gave Benjamin a long stare. 'Walker won't accept being humiliated.'

'I know, and if he tries anything I'll defend myself, but I won't humiliate him and I won't seek him out to best him again.'

If Benjamin had claimed he wouldn't cause trouble no matter what Walker did, Cassidy wouldn't have believed him, but he liked the honesty of his answer.

He slapped his shoulder. 'See that you don't and you'll be fine. Break that promise and you'll end up in a cell.'

After hearing that encouragement and warning, Benjamin left the saloon, leaving Floyd to come down the bar to join Cassidy.

'I'm not sure you did the right thing there,' he said.

'I won't get any trouble from Benjamin and I trust Leland to deal with Walker himself.'

'Maybe, but if anyone other than the son of Leland Matlock had gone for a concealed gun, would you have let him walk out of here a free man?'

Cassidy frowned. Slowly he sipped his drink.

After fifteen minutes of brooding silence he nodded and straightened up.

'You're right,' he said. He left the bar and headed outside with a determined tread. He set off for Leland Matlock's house, considering how he would deal with the difficult task ahead.

A man was standing on the edge of town outside the building. He was smoking while looking out of town, but when he sensed Cassidy approaching, he flicked the cheroot to the ground and walked away. By the time Cassidy reached the door, the man had mounted up and was riding away.

Cassidy considered him, but then he heard a person approach from behind. He turned to find himself facing Millicent.

'So you're doing nothing,' she snapped.

Cassidy winced. They hadn't shared a civil word in six months and from the tone of her voice, it didn't sound as if that was about to change.

'I'm going to talk to Leland.' He offered a smile.

'You're already too late,' she said, her tone gruff

and her eyes glistening in the low light, perhaps from crying. 'Walker and Leland argued. I know you'd never do anything I ask you to, but—'

'My feelings don't matter when I'm keeping the peace. If you reckon Walker will harm Benjamin, I need to know about it.'

Millicent snorted, shaking her head. 'That proves you'll never help. The problem isn't Walker; it's Benjamin. His terrible lies make me think he'll harm Walker.'

Cassidy considered whether he should discuss those lies with her, but he accepted he did only have Benjamin's word for what had been going on.

'Where are they?' he asked.

'Benjamin followed Walker out of town.' She pointed, indicating a route between the railroad tracks and the river.

'Don't worry. I'll find them and make sure nobody comes to harm.'

'Then do it,' she said, her tone containing a hurtful amount of scepticism.

He tipped his hat then hurried to his horse.

Two minutes later he rode out of town. Millicent watched him go and as if in confirmation of her story, Leland came to the window and looked at him.

He trotted along beside the railroad tracks, searching ahead for signs of either man. He was four miles out of town when for the first time movement caught his eye.

He looked towards the river and in the low moonlight he saw that the movement had come from Riker's Bend, a rise that had created a long curve in the river.

This area provided pleasant memories because when he and Millicent had been together they had often come here to picnic. But tonight the rise presented a dark, forbidding mass and on the top of the rise a standing man was silhouetted against the sky before he disappeared from view.

Cassidy headed for the river. He tethered his horse to an oak then climbed the rise.

When he looked over the top he saw Benjamin sitting on a boulder by the riverside, his outline stark. He was throwing stones into the river with long sweeps of his arm, working off his anger.

At the base of the rise and out of Benjamin's view, the heavy-set Walker was moving stealthily towards him in the shadows.

Clearly the confrontation that Millicent had feared was about to take place but not in the way she'd envisaged.

Cassidy considered making his presence known, but despite Millicent's concern, he didn't expect either man to harm the other seriously. So while Walker continued to move towards Benjamin, he swung over the top of the rise and made his way down to ground level silently and in the shadows.

He was nearing ground level when Walker dislodged a stone and this made Benjamin stand, a hand rising to his brow as he peered into the darkness.

'Is that you, Walker?' he demanded.

Walker grunted an oath as he emerged from the shadow of the rise.

Benjamin faced the approaching man. He muttered a reply that Cassidy couldn't hear. They traded insults. An argument raged with much finger-pointing and posturing.

Cassidy speeded his approach. As the men closed on each other he reached ground level and walked quickly towards them.

He was thirty yards away when a stray beam of light flashed off an object in Benjamin's hand that had the sheen of gunmetal. Cassidy broke into a run, a warning on his lips, but a gunshot blasted.

An agonized cry rent the air.

Walker doubled over. He took a pace towards the river. Then he fell into the water.

Cassidy shouted out a plea for calm that made Benjamin look at him. Walker was now lying face down in the water and drifting away.

Benjamin turned and broke into a run, fleeing into the shadows. When Cassidy reached the scene of the shooting Walker was ten feet away, his form swirling round as the current grabbed hold.

Cassidy decided that saving Walker's life was more important than chasing Benjamin. He waded into the river until the breathtakingly cold water rose up to his waist, but he was already too late. Walker's body had caught a strong current and it was drifting out into the centre of the river.

Seeing no other choice, Cassidy gave up on his rescue attempt and returned to dry land.

Within minutes he was riding down river, but when he failed to catch sight of the body again, he headed into town to instruct Deputy Wright to arrest Benjamin while he organized a proper search.

As it turned out, Benjamin gave himself up without a fight, but after the search party failed to find Walker's body, the aftermath of the incident at Riker's Bend spiralled into disaster.

For differing reasons the two most influential men in town doubted Cassidy's actions.

With the help of the best lawyers he could hire Benjamin's father Stanley fought to prove his son hadn't killed Walker. As there was no body and only one witness, Cassidy's testimony was vital, but the lawyers couldn't shake him from it.

Cassidy knew what he'd seen. At the trial the integrity of a lawman persuaded the jury of Benjamin's guilt. He got life.

Afterwards the distraught mayor wouldn't talk to the town founder, an unhealthy situation in a formerly friendly town, but that was as nothing compared to his loathing for the sheriff. He didn't speak to Cassidy again.

As for Leland, despite seeing justice done, he directed his anger at Cassidy, the man who had failed to lock up Benjamin. He had been wrong to let an argument develop in the saloon. He was the only one who'd seen Walker draw a gun. He hadn't stopped Benjamin killing Walker.

Cassidy knew that Leland's grief made him say these things, so he didn't contradict him, but even though Leland failed to destroy the confidence of the townsfolk in their sheriff completely, enough people began doubting him.

Cassidy's days as sheriff were numbered.

A year later when Stanley Shaw again stood for mayor, Edwin Johanson stood successfully with him for sheriff.

Despite this, Cassidy had clung on to his belief that he had been right, summed up by the comment that again came to his lips as he finished reviewing those events.

'I know what I saw.'

CHAPTER 5

Cassidy set off at first light, aiming to cover the remaining thirty miles to Destitution, the first town along the tracks, that day.

Unfortunately, last night his pondering hadn't provided him with any additional clues to work out what was happening. Aside from Elizabeth's death and Leland's attack both happening at the Shaw Hotel, he had no reason to connect them to each other or to connect them to the events of last year, other than a hunch.

This didn't stop him mulling over the events, as he'd done when he'd been a lawman, but two hours into the day a more important consideration drove those thoughts from his mind.

He was being followed.

The problem had begun as that old feeling in which he was sure someone was looking at him combined with the back of his neck burning.

Later, when he rode over a small rise he stopped and glanced around. About a half-mile back he saw movement and a puff of dust as presumably whoever was following him went to ground.

Cassidy speeded to a trot reaching an area in which boulders were strewn over the route ahead. He picked out two large boulders and rode between them.

On seeing the open ground beyond, he veered to the side. He jumped down from his horse and tethered it, then climbed up the largest of the boulders.

The boulder was fifteen feet high letting him lie on the flat top without being seen. On his belly he shuffled to the edge and listened.

Presently the clop of horses' hoofs approached. He discerned three sets of hoofbeats. He waited until the sounds changed tone as the horses passed through the gap, then got to his knees and peered down.

Three men were riding by, all having the down-cast postures of men making a long journey. One man was Dodge Elwood, the man who'd tried to make him sign the petition yesterday. Behind him was Zachary McKinney.

He didn't recognize the lead man and this man would see Cassidy's horse when he emerged from the gap. So Cassidy raised himself to his feet and when Dodge was below him he jumped.

His shadow flickered on the ground, catching

Dodge's attention, but he was too late to stop Cassidy crashing down on to his shoulders and dragging him from his horse.

Dodge landed on his back with Cassidy using him to break his fall then rolling over a shoulder before he came to a halt. He jumped to his feet and drew his gun as the other men swung their horses round to face him.

'Reach,' he muttered, making the mounted men thrust their hands high. Dodge lay on his back with his eyes closed, groaning.

Cassidy took no chances and dragged Dodge's gun from its holster then threw it away. Then he signified that the mounted men should dismount and throw their weaponry to the ground.

Zachary complied with a smirk on his lips that said the situation didn't concern him. But after Cassidy gave him a knowing look, he removed a second gun from his jacket. The other man shook his head and opened his jacket to show he didn't carry a gun.

'Why did you attack us?' he asked, using a calm and cultured tone as he jumped down from his horse.

'Why are you following me?' Cassidy snapped. 'Whoever you are.'

'I'm Vincent Pershing.' He paused as if Cassidy should know the name. 'I'm Mayor Stanley Shaw's attorney.'

'Then I wish you luck in finding new employ-

58

ment.' Cassidy smiled. 'Stanley's lawyers don't last long.'

Vincent's placid expression didn't change.

'We don't need to at the rates he pays. And now I'm earning my pay by going where you're going' – Vincent widened his eyes, enjoying his revelation – 'in search of information about Elizabeth Caine.'

Cassidy narrowed his eyes. 'What do you know about her?'

'Nothing other than the fact you're investigating Leland's shooting and you deemed her murder as being significant.'

'Then you've wasted a journey. There's nothing to prove her death had anything to do with Leland's shooting and nothing to connect it to your client's plea for clemency.'

Vincent provided a confident snort of laughter.

'There isn't, other than the look in your eyes that says you reckon they're connected, except you don't know how yet. I intend to be there when you make that connection.'

Cassidy shrugged then looked at Zachary.

'And your reason for following me?'

'I do what Millicent Matlock pays me to do.' Zachary folded his arms, presenting an unconcerned air.

Judging that he wouldn't get any helpful answers from him, Cassidy turned to Dodge, who was stirring and rubbing his forehead.

'Stanley wants your signature on his petition,' Dodge murmured as he sat up.

Cassidy sneered. 'Then you're wasting your time too.'

He considered the men. Dodge was groggy and would need time to get his senses about him. He'd bested Zachary once before, and the unarmed Vincent was a typical lawyer and unlikely to be trouble.

He was minded to get on his horse and leave them behind in a flurry of trail dust, but on the other hand, if he stayed with them he could watch what they did. So he headed to his horse and mounted up.

'Then stop standing around enjoying the scenery,' he said. 'I've not got the time to waste.'

Throughout the sultry afternoon Cassidy set a brisk pace, neither acknowledging his unwanted companions nor showing any outward signs that their presence annoyed him.

But as the day wore on the intriguing thought that they might have joined him for reasons other than what they had claimed overtook his irritation. Maybe the fact that Elizabeth had died in Stanley Shaw's hotel *was* significant, after all.

So he bided his time, waiting for them to make a mistake. But by the time the sun was lowering it had became clear that although Dodge and Zachary filled the journey with idle chatter, they were unlikely to reveal anything interesting. They were following someone else's orders and it was probable that they knew nothing about Elizabeth.

The only one who was acting on his own initiative was Vincent and he kept any information he'd gathered hidden beneath layers of studied professional conduct.

Late in the day they rode into Destitution. Cassidy found an old friend in the saloon and with Dodge and Zachary at his side he asked him if he knew Elizabeth Caine or anyone matching her description who had left town recently.

The friend hadn't heard of her. Neither had anyone else he asked. So they stayed for the night in the town's only hotel, then moved on the next morning.

They reached Bitter Creek late in the afternoon where Cassidy carried out the same routine, again without luck.

That lack of success continued for the next two days as the mismatched group settled into a routine.

They set off early and at a steady pace they rode on. Their journey was silent except when it was interrupted by Zachary's and Dodge's chatter. They reached the next station along the tracks, usually arriving late in the afternoon. Cassidy asked around, but learnt nothing, after which they settled in a hotel for the night and set off early the next day for the next town with a station.

Cassidy was sure this method would work as Elizabeth had to have come from somewhere, but his companions were less sure.

On the fifth day of their journey Dodge and Zachary started offering wild suggestions for how they could find out where she'd come from more efficiently. Cassidy smiled when for the first time Vincent's cool demeanour cracked and he snapped at his companions to be quiet.

Sundown was an hour away when they rode into Bear Creek. As usual Cassidy and his companions went into the largest saloon, but this time he didn't question anyone. Cassidy had a source of information here that was better than most and he didn't want to squander the opportunity while he could be overheard.

They sat at a table and drank coffee. Presently Vincent raised the question of where they'd stay tonight.

'I'll ask about rooms,' Cassidy said then left the table and headed to the bar.

As the long day of simmering tension had dulled everybody's senses, nobody followed him and so he was alone when he caught the gaze of the bartender Curtis Samuels.

'Not seen you around these parts recently,' Curtis said. His gaze darted down to look at Cassidy's jacket where a star had once sat and he flashed a sympathetic smile. 'Who're your companions?'

Cassidy glanced over his shoulder at the table where the three men were casting irritated glances at each other.

'Shadows,' he said. 'So quickly: do you know Elizabeth Caine?'

'Sure, everyone knows her.' Curtis provided a knowing look that said Deputy Wright had been correct about her occupation. 'But she's not in town.'

Cassidy noted that news of her demise hadn't reached Bear Creek.

'When did she leave?'

'Not sure. Ask Belle Carter. Elizabeth works for her.' Curtis paused to rub his chin then leaned towards Cassidy and lowered his voice. 'And you're not the only person who's interested in her.'

Cassidy nodded, acknowledging the strictures under which Curtis operated. He was a reliable source of information, but he was also free with its spreading. Their friendship forced him to stretch the rules that had been set for him, so that he decided to let Cassidy know that someone wanted to be told about anyone asking about her.

Footfalls approached and Curtis flicked him a significant glance, so Cassidy limited himself to grunting his thanks. He turned and barged past Dodge and Zachary.

'You get us a room?' Vincent asked when he arrived back at the table.

'Decided not to ask,' Cassidy said.

'Then did you find out anything about Elizabeth Caine?'

'Nope. So I'm moving on. I'll never get to the truth unless I speed up.' Cassidy turned to the door, but then he turned back and smiled. 'Not that you have to face a night under the stars. You can stay here.'

Vincent considered Cassidy's amused gaze. A confident smile appeared, accepting the challenge of the game they would play in which Cassidy would try to wear him down.

'I've faced better men than you in a courtroom and won,' he said. 'I'll stay with you until you get to the truth.'

Cassidy shrugged then left the saloon without further word.

Vincent may have been taciturn but Dodge more than made up for his lack of complaints. As they rode out of town, he started a litany of mutterings about where they'd be sleeping tonight that didn't let up until Vincent ordered him to quieten.

Feeling in a more contented frame of mind, Cassidy considered his companions that night when they'd settled down, through the flickering flames of the campfire.

'So,' he said, 'why are you really shadowing me?'

Dodge and Zachary glanced at each other, but both men said nothing and let Vincent speak.

64

'We're seeing what your private investigation uncovers.'

Cassidy leaned forward. 'Who does your client suspect Elizabeth was before she was murdered in his hotel?'

Vincent matched Cassidy's movement by leaning forward.

'What do *you* suspect?'

Cassidy sneered and turned to Zachary, deciding that trading words with a lawyer who devoted his life to misrepresenting the truth was a futile exercise.

'What about you?' he said. 'I don't believe Millicent would hire you to protect Leland from Stanley Shaw, then tell you to follow me with the lawyer Stanley hired to represent Benjamin.'

Vincent coughed, noting that Cassidy had changed the subject in an unsubtle manner.

'I do what I'm paid to do and I don't ask unnecessary questions,' Zachary said. He smirked, but Cassidy didn't reply and sure enough he filled the silence. 'But if I did, I'd conclude that Stanley and Benjamin aren't the only ones who hate Leland. Finding answers with you might lead me to whoever shot him.'

Cassidy conceded this explanation with a nod then turned to Dodge.

'Why are you wasting so much time in pursuit of another signature?'

'The mayor,' Dodge said, grinning, 'will pay

plenty for your signature.'

'He would, but why didn't you just get someone to forge it?'

Dodge provided a guilty look, confirming that he'd considered doing this and that presumably other signatures had already been obtained this way.

'This time I'll wait for a real signature.'

The honest answer made Cassidy shake his head then look at Vincent.

'Aren't you bothered about where those signatures came from?' he asked. 'It'll weaken your case if anyone's suspects they're not what they seem.'

Vincent's resolute gaze didn't flicker.

'Of course they're not what they seem,' he said. 'The governor knows that the size of the petition is merely a sign of the determination of the men who've lined up behind Benjamin Shaw's appeal, and of the trouble we'll cause if he doesn't accede to our wishes.'

Cassidy smiled. 'Was Elizabeth's death a hint of that trouble?'

Vincent flinched then raised himself to poke the fire.

'Who's taking the first watch?' he said, looking through the flames at Cassidy.

Cassidy coughed, ensuring Vincent understood he had noticed his abrupt change of subject. He stood and headed to his saddle and blanket.

'I'm not interested. I reckon we're safe here and

a good night's sleep will be of more use.' Cassidy slipped under his blanket, but then he sat bolt upright and swirled round as if a sudden thought had hit him. 'Unless you know we're being followed.'

Vincent ignored him, but Cassidy noted the worried glance he shot at Dodge and Zachary. While they agreed amongst themselves that Zachary would take the first watch, Cassidy settled down under his blanket and within minutes he'd drifted off into a contented sleep.

The four men had settled down some hours ago.

Rockwell Trent had watched them for long enough to confirm that only one man was on watch. An hour ago they had changed that watch and the new man was lying still.

The men in the camp were silent except for the occasional sleepy stirring and they were showing no sign of being alert enough to spot him approaching. Rockwell hadn't been told why he needed to follow these men then sneak into their camp, but as usual he hadn't asked for a reason.

He had dismissed as an odd coincidence his recent setbacks of twice finding the person he'd been hired to kill already dead. Now he was enjoying being able to employ the skills he'd prided himself on honing to perfection.

In the group one man appeared to be leading although Rockwell's distant observation led him to believe he was a reluctant leader. When they'd settled down he'd crept close enough to recognize him as being Cassidy Yates, a man he'd seen but never confronted before.

This discovery had added extra piquancy to his mission and had made him decide to abandon his trademark method of dispatch in favour of a silent knife slash across the throat.

The man keeping watch would be the first to die and once he'd been dispatched silently, Cassidy would be next. The other two wouldn't last for long.

Rockwell dropped to his knees and crawled towards the watch's position, keeping in the shadows until he was ten paces away from his target.

The journey took five minutes and yet Rockwell didn't make a sound, avoiding any stray twigs or pebbles. Even his breathing was controlled enough to be nothing more than a whisper, but the same couldn't be said for his quarry.

Rockwell heard the rasping snores that said the only danger this man would present would come from him delivering a sudden waking shout before he silenced him.

Rockwell resolved not to give him that chance. He stood and stealthily made his way towards the prone man. He placed each foot to the ground silently, emerging gradually from the shadows.

He was counting down the paces while mentally

rehearsing the movements he'd make of clamping a hand over the man's mouth and ripping the knife under his chin when a feeling of wrongness overcame him.

This instinct had saved him before and he'd always heeded it.

He stopped and cocked his head to one side as he tried to work out what the problem was.

It came to him. While he'd been approaching his quarry the snoring hadn't increased in volume, so the man wasn't the one who was snoring. Someone down in the camp was fast asleep and the sound was drifting up the slope.

'You're slipping,' Rockwell murmured to himself, his error rattling him. Then his heart pounded in annoyance on realizing he'd let his irritation bubble over and he'd made an unnecessary sound.

Eager now to get this over with quickly he paced with steady determination to the prone man, stood over him, and with practised stealth he carried out his rehearsed motion.

He swooped. One hand grabbed the man's chin, covering the mouth, and the other swung under the bared neck, but stickiness on his left hand halted him. The man's head lolled as if the neck lacked the muscles to hold it up.

Rockwell flinched back, peering at his hand. Blood glistened in the starlight.

Without heed to the noise he made he kicked

the man over on to his back. His exposed, sliced neck arched backwards, showing an inhumanly wide grin that seemed to mock him with silent laughter.

The man had already been killed in the same manner that Rockwell had planned to use.

'What the—?' Rockwell grunted as he stared into the man's blank eyes. In his bemused state he kicked a stone and sent it skittering down the slope towards the camp.

The sudden noise silenced the snoring below. On the light evening breeze the murmuring of people asking whether they'd heard a noise reached him, but Rockwell was rooted to the spot.

No longer could he dismiss the bizarre events of the last few weeks as coincidences. Someone was picking off his intended targets before he could get to them.

Worse, his current mission could no longer be finished stealthily. Only a few weeks ago Rockwell would have shrugged off the misfortune of alerting his victims and gone on to dispatch them from the shadows, but now.

Something was wrong and Rockwell no longer trusted his skill. He backed away from the body, speeding his retreat and by the time he heard the shocked sounds of the group discovering the dead man, he had reached his horse.

He mounted up and rode away. The night air rushed by, but it failed to cool his sweating brow, and no matter how hard he clutched the reins he couldn't stop his hands from shaking.

CHAPTER 6

Cassidy peered into the darkness from behind his two covering boulders and considered his limited field of vision.

Having found that Dodge had been killed, his throat slashed, he had taken the safest option by retiring into cover behind their campsite. For the last hour he'd waited for whoever was out there to come for him.

Earlier, Zachary had decided the killer had gone and he was sitting hunched beside the fire as if staying warm would keep him alive. Vincent had gone off on a foolhardy scouting mission to find the killer.

Cassidy didn't expect to see him alive again.

Despite Cassidy's pessimism the rest of the night passed slowly and, as it turned out, whoever had attacked them didn't come back. Cassidy still waited until it was fully light before he ventured back to Dodge's body. Then he searched for signs of the killer's passage, finding after some searching that he'd headed away from Bear Creek.

The route Vincent had taken was easier to follow. Despite his last words, in which in an uncharacteristic act he'd promised to track down Dodge's killer if it were the last thing he did, he'd reverted to character and his hurried direction was towards Bear Creek.

When Cassidy returned to the campsite he headed to his horse.

'I plan to travel fast until I've thrown the killer off my trail,' he called over his shoulder as he mounted up. 'So talk to me or I'll leave you to make your own way to safety.'

'Hey,' Zachary shouted, hurrying up to him, 'we need to stick together.'

'We don't, and look at it this way, if you're sure nobody's after you, I must be the target. You'll be safer without me.'

'Perhaps I will. But those aren't my orders.' When Cassidy raised the reins as if he'd leave in a hurry, Zachary's shoulders slumped and he rubbed his furrowed brow, appearing as if he was debating something with himself. He looked up. 'All right, I'll tell you what I know, but it won't help.'

Cassidy gestured to Zachary's horse, inviting him to mount up and join him. At a walking pace they left the campsite.

'Go on,' Cassidy said when they reached the plains and were heading away from Bear Creek.

Zachary rode on for a minute silently. When he did speak, his low tone had an honest ring to it.

'I'm not a hired gun. I'm an investigator. Millicent hired me because Leland was convinced Benjamin Shaw would be freed soon. I was to find out why and to stop it happening.'

'Why would that killer get out?'

'The story I pieced together is that Elizabeth Caine contacted Stanley Shaw. She said she had information that'd help Benjamin. Stanley paid and for the next few months she eked out a few tasty morsels. Don't ask me how I know this.'

'I don't need to know the details of how much you paid Vincent Pershing to talk.'

Zachary snorted a laugh, as if to say his guess was wrong, although his furtive cough before he spoke again only went to suggest he had been close to the truth.

'Stanley's former lawyer dealt with her and Stanley wondered if it were a trick. He hired Vincent and he was more hard-nosed. He offered her an all-or-nothing deal. In return she claimed that for a thousand dollars she'd provide conclusive evidence that Benjamin didn't kill Walker Matlock.'

Cassidy couldn't help but shake his head.

'And Stanley believed that nonsense?'

'He did. Vincent said he'd only pay her if she came to Monotony and presented her evidence face-to-face. But someone killed her before anyone found out what she knew.'

'Or killed her after finding out what she knew.' Cassidy glanced at Zachary. 'And the people who wouldn't want that information divulged would be the Matlock family and by extension you.'

Zachary shrugged. 'When she died I was under arrest and Millicent was looking after Leland.'

'Then who could it be?'

Zachary considered before he answered.

'I don't know, but I'd guess her killer was the man who really killed Walker Matlock.'

Cassidy frowned. 'An interesting tale, except I know what I saw that night. Benjamin killed Walker.'

'You heard a gunshot and saw Walker die. But someone else could have been in the shadows.'

Cassidy firmed his jaw, unwilling to accept this possibility.

'I know what I saw!'

Without further comment Cassidy drew his horse to a halt, swung it round, and headed back towards Bear Creek.

Zachary started to ask why he'd changed direction. Then he uttered a loud sigh and when he caught up with Cassidy he gave him a rueful smile.

'I shouldn't have left you alone,' he said.

At noon Cassidy was sitting alone beside the window in a hotel room in Bear Creek pondering.

They'd seen nothing untoward on the return journey to Bear Creek. When they'd arrived in town Zachary hadn't complained when he'd suggested they needed to get out of sight for a while.

Although his old friend Curtis didn't deal with booking people into the hotel that adjoined the saloon, Cassidy had still told him of his plans to stay.

Night had fallen when the expected knock came at the door. Cassidy stood and moved to stand side-on to the door. He drew his gun then bade his visitor to enter.

The door opened to reveal a woman, who identified herself as Belle Carter. Her eyes registered only amusement at the sight of his drawn gun, suggesting Curtis had already warned her.

'You asked about Elizabeth Caine,' she said.

Cassidy nodded and holstered his gun. He sat then signified that she should sit on the other side of the window facing him.

'I did, and I'm sorry.' Cassidy lowered his tone to a sympathetic one. 'She's dead.'

Belle winced and looked through the window, her minimal reaction suggesting this revelation hadn't surprised her. When she asked him to explain, he gave her a brief summary of the details, after which she murmured to herself that Elizabeth had been a fool before she raised her voice.

'She's almost as popular when dead,' she said, 'as alive.'

'Who else asked about her?'

Belle's response was to stand then head to the door while beckoning him to follow.

She took him up a flight of stairs to a hall where the rest of Belle's girls worked. But when she reached the top of the stairs a shriek escaped her lips and she came to a sudden halt.

From behind her Cassidy saw that the door at the end of the hall had been kicked down. He told her to stay back then hurried on. He backhanded the remnants of the door open to see that the room was unoccupied, but it had been ransacked with clothes strewn around and furniture toppled.

'He didn't give a name,' Belle said, looking past him to consider the mess. 'But he was thin and furtive.'

'Vincent Pershing,' Cassidy muttered with irritation.

Rockwell's quarry was ten paces ahead and this time he wouldn't get away.

The last few hours had been uncomfortable.

Rockwell had never had to make excuses before, but in this case he'd had no choice but to report he'd failed. He had claimed that Dodge had cried out and alerted Cassidy Yates and the other men in the camp so he'd been unable to dispatch them.

Now he was determined to put that unfortunate matter behind him.

Vincent Pershing was making his way down the road away from the hotel, moving into the less frequented part of town. Rockwell silently placed his feet to the boardwalk as he awaited the right moment to move.

Few people were about. Two men were walking away on the other side of the road and one man was approaching Vincent. Rockwell decided he would wait until that person had passed him, then speed up to catch up with his quarry.

But when the person had passed him, Vincent stopped then glanced over his shoulder. His gaze fell on Rockwell.

This had rarely happened before. His quarries never usually heard him approach until it was too late. Often they never heard him at all. Now Vincent was looking at him and his shocked gaze showed that he'd identified him as someone who was following him.

Vincent took another pace while looking around, confirming that few people were about. Then he ran.

Rockwell gave up on any pretence of not pursuing him and broke into a run. He pounded down the road then across it when Vincent veered away.

The stables were on the edge of town and Rockwell presumed that Vincent was heading there. Then, with an angry slap of a hand against his thigh, he realized that he hadn't checked where Vincent had left his horse.

Angry now at his mistake Rockwell speeded up to run as fast as he could. From the corner of his eye he saw the people on the other side of the road look at them with bemused interest, but Rockwell was beyond caring whether he was seen or not.

His only objective was to catch Vincent and kill him.

Vincent was running down the boardwalk, five yards ahead and the stables were another fifty yards beyond. He glanced over his shoulder at Rockwell, his shocked and red face registering his disappointment at how close Rockwell was. His lumbering paces said he wouldn't reach the stables in time and Rockwell was starting to relax when unexpectedly Vincent swerved to the left and ran into an alley.

Rockwell knew that the only exits on either side of this alley were the doors to the surrounding mercantile and bank.

Five seconds after Vincent disappeared from view Rockwell followed him into the alley. But then he had to dive to the ground, only his lightning reactions letting him avoid a stone that whistled over his back.

Rockwell hit the ground on his chest with his arms swinging out to hold his gun at arm's length. He fired at the form ahead, not giving Vincent a second chance to attack him. Lead slammed into Vincent's chest sending him tumbling.

A satisfied grunt escaped Rockwell lips as he tore a second bullet into him.

Even as Vincent writhed in his final fatal dance

Rockwell was on his feet and hurrying to him. He stood over him and then emptied round after round into Vincent's body.

'Got you,' he grunted as he reloaded to slam more bullets into the dead body.

Even several more rounds didn't assuage his anger and he reached for his knife planning to carve the body, as he would have done last night. But then sense overcame the bloodlust and he backed away from the body then hurried to the alley entrance.

He glanced up and down the road. The people who had been nearby had decided to be elsewhere while lead was flying, leaving the road deserted.

Rockwell took one last look at the body, shivered, then headed off to track down the others.

'He was seen heading this way,' Cassidy said as he approached the stables.

'He shouldn't have tried to find Elizabeth on his own,' Zachary McKinney said, for not the first time.

'Men like Vincent know that information is money.'

Zachary sighed. 'Then maybe he paid in the worst possible way. They say the gunfire came from over here.'

Cassidy nodded and when they'd confirmed that Vincent's horse was still in the stables, he was even surer. They retraced their steps, but they didn't need to go far. In the first alley he looked into Cassidy saw a hunched body.

With Zachary at his side he slipped into the alley. Closer to, he saw the dark patch of dirt glistening around the body and when he rolled it over he flinched back in shock. The victim had been subjected to a frenzied assault and he had to drag the body into a patch of light to see the pitted face and confirm its identity.

'It's Vincent,' Cassidy said, stepping back to let Zachary look.

Cassidy waited, but when Zachary didn't respond he glanced up. Zachary wasn't visible.

Cassidy looked around. It was too dark to see anything other than the thin sliver of the road beyond the end of the alley, but then he heard a footfall. He started to turn but he was already too late.

From behind a hand flicked his gun from its holster. A second hand clamped around his neck, the fingers icy cold.

'Don't move,' a voice muttered in his ear.

'What do you want?' Cassidy murmured.

His assailant swirled him round, letting him see the dark mass of Zachary's form standing a few feet beyond the body with his hands raised. From further down the alley a man was walking towards them, his form just an outline in the low light.

The man stopped with his face still masked by shadows.

'Cassidy Yates,' he said, 'why are you asking about Elizabeth Caine?'

The voice was familiar and Cassidy searched his memory to place it.

'I'm investigating an assault on Leland Matlock in Monotony.'

The man uttered a low grunt, perhaps of surprise, perhaps of approval.

'Are you using the same diligence for that investigation as you did for your investigation into Walker Matlock's murder?'

Something about the way the man said that name tapped at Cassidy's memory, but he dismissed the possibility with a shrug.

'I know what I saw that night.'

'You saw what you wanted to see, but answer my question. What has Elizabeth got to do with this assault on Leland?'

'I reckon Leland and Elizabeth are connected to the events of last year.'

'Enough to prove that Benjamin Shaw is innocent?'

'Zachary here believes that Elizabeth had that proof.'

'But you don't?' The man waited until Cassidy shook his head, then snorted. 'If you still believe that Benjamin killed Walker, you're still as pathetic as you were when you were a lawman.'

The man stepped out of the shadows to stand in a patch of light and despite the previous hint

about his identity, Cassidy couldn't help but gasp.
The man was Walker Matlock.

CHAPTER 7

'I know what I saw,' Cassidy murmured for what would probably be the last time.

He had never doubted that what he'd seen last year was Benjamin Shaw killing Walker Matlock, but now the 'dead' man was standing before him.

Walker's guard Rockwell Trent still held Cassidy securely and he flashed Walker a glance, requesting instructions on what he should do next.

Walker returned a shake of the head that Cassidy presumed was an order not to kill him, although his cold-eyed stare left him in no doubt that the order was a delay and not a reprieve.

'Tell me about this attack on my father,' Walker said.

'It's a long story,' Cassidy said. 'Perhaps we should discuss it in my hotel room.'

Walker glanced at the body of Vincent Pershing then raised his head as if listening for anyone approaching. He nodded, accepting that their discovery could be imminent.

'Elizabeth's room will be better.' Walker offered a smile without warmth. 'You can clear up the mess this one made.'

Walker gestured for Rockwell to release him then for Cassidy to take the lead. Rockwell pushed the reluctant Zachary towards the alley entrance. In silence they headed to the hotel.

On the way Cassidy tried to think through the implications of this unexpected development, but the shock was too great and his mind remained resolutely blank.

When they arrived at Elizabeth's room Belle Carter was tidying up, but she took one look at Walker and Rockwell then scurried away.

While Rockwell and Walker stood by the door, Cassidy and Zachary went to the window where Cassidy caught Zachary's eye. If the investigator was pleased with the confirmation that the clues he'd uncovered were correct, he didn't show it. Instead he returned a worried look.

Walker invited Cassidy to speak with a raised eyebrow.

'A few days ago your father got shot in an alley,' Cassidy said, 'in the same way that Vincent died.'

The dead-eyed Rockwell didn't react and Walker took this news with barely a flicker in his cold gaze.

'Why are you investigating this after they voted you out of office?'

'Your father and I haven't spoken since you . . .

you died, but before his assault he had something important to tell me. I had to find out what that was.'

Walker snorted. 'My father would never speak to you after what you did to our family.'

Cassidy struggled to find a response that would placate Walker, leaving Zachary to answer the question Cassidy had thought Walker would ask.

'The shooting left your father in a serious condition,' he said. 'I don't know if he'll be alive when we return.'

Walker shrugged before he knelt then picked up a pile of discarded clothing. He placed the items on the bed then folded them with more care than Cassidy would have expected from a man such as the surly Walker.

'I'm obliged for the information,' he said with a significant glance at Rockwell, 'but why did this investigation lead you to Elizabeth?'

Previously Cassidy had got the impression that Walker had only asked questions to which he knew the answer, but no longer. As with surprising tenderness Walker tidied Elizabeth's strewn clothes, Cassidy made the connection he'd been struggling to make since he'd found the torn up letter in the alley where Leland had been shot.

'I'm sorry,' he said, lowering his tone, 'but I only found out that your mother had come to Monotony after she'd been killed.'

Walker snapped his head up to glare at him, but

when Cassidy gave a firm nod he gulped then slumped down to sprawl on the bed. He righted himself but his head was still bowed as he picked up a kerchief from the bed and cradled it for a moment before he flung it away.

When he spoke again his voice emerged as a strangulated plea.

'Who?'

'I don't know, yet. So help me. Tell me what you've done since I saw you fall into the river with a bullet in your guts.'

'Rockwell got me out,' Walker murmured, his tone hollow and distracted. 'Then I licked my wounds and stayed out of the reach of that murderous son of Stanley Shaw. Elizabeth took me in.'

'You already knew about her?'

'Father claimed she was dead, but I found the letters.'

'Who else knew about her?'

Walker looked up and raised an eyebrow, offering a smile for the first time since Cassidy's revelation.

'That's good thinking. Only the early settlers would have known about her, such as Stanley Shaw, Edwin Johanson, Judge Mitchell. . . .'

'Would they have known why she left?'

A pained look overcame Walker's eyes as he shook his head. 'I tire of your questions and I need to think this through, so I'll make this simple for you.' Walker flared his eyes and took deep breaths.

'I'm going back to Monotony. When we return you'll find her killer or Rockwell will find you.'

The sun was at its highest when Cassidy saw Monotony again.

Despite the presence of his latest collection of unwanted companions the journey had been an uneventful one.

On the outskirts of Monotony Walker ordered Rockwell to stay out of town and without complaint the Iceman drew his horse away. Then, with Walker trailing along behind, Zachary and Cassidy rode on for what Cassidy expected would be the oddest homecoming he'd ever seen.

Few people were about and as they passed them they all gave the riders barely a glance, not that anyone would expect a dead man to ride back into town.

When they were halfway down the road Zachary turned to Cassidy.

'I reckon,' he said, 'that with Rockwell being here Millicent won't require my services no more. So perhaps I should ingratiate myself with Stanley.'

'It's worth a try,' Cassidy said. 'And someone has to tell him the news. It'd sound better coming from someone other than me.'

Zachary tipped his hat then hurried on to the hotel without a backward glance. When he disappeared inside Cassidy turned in the saddle to face Walker, who with a shrug drew his horse to a halt.

He looked down the road at his home on the far edge of town then considered Cassidy.

'This is where we part company,' he said.

'Sure,' Cassidy said. 'I really do hope your father's condition has improved and that your unexpected return raises his spirits.'

'Strangely, so do I. He's all I have left now.'

'There is Millicent.'

'There is,' Walker said, although he didn't sound pleased with the thought of being reunited with his wife. He carried on down the road.

Cassidy watched him leave, seeing several people cast him odd looks before they dismissed the sighting.

Walker had reached his father's house when Zachary came bustling out of the hotel with Stanley Shaw in tow. Like Leland, Stanley hadn't spoken to him in a year, but he came running over.

'Is it true?' he asked eagerly as if the last year had never happened.

Cassidy provided a rueful smile.

'Yes,' he said. 'So I'll sign your petition. Your son didn't kill Walker Matlock. I was wrong.'

With that admission he turned his horse around and trotted out of town towards his home.

Behind him Stanley hooted and hollered with glee.

CHAPTER 8

The bunting was already out.

The sight made Cassidy draw up on the edge of town to consider if he wanted to ride on. Then at a slower pace he continued down the road.

For the last week he'd stayed away, hoping that his absence after his apology might help to heal the rifts in town. He was mindful of Walker's ultimatum, but he also hoped that Sheriff Edwin Johanson might have made progress in finding out who had killed Elizabeth Caine.

He also hoped the answer would help to bring the Matlock and Shaw families together before Benjamin was released and he and Walker found themselves living in the same town again.

When Cassidy dismounted beside the saloon he saw that hotel workers were erecting a podium outside the Shaw Hotel, and Cassidy was pleased that when they saw his interest they nodded and waved. This reaction was better than the one he'd been worried about receiving from men who worked for the mayor.

Heartened he turned to the Silver Streak. He noted that the increased activity and gaiety out on the road wasn't affecting everyone.

Outside the saloon there were a dozen men, each being rough-clad and trail-dirty, and they were eyeing the work with studied uninterest. Cassidy didn't recognize any of them and that alone removed his contented mood.

He carried on past the saloon and glanced into the law office. To his irritation Johanson was sitting at his desk, his posture, hunched over in his chair, being the same as the one he'd adopted when he'd last seen him two weeks ago.

So Cassidy headed back to his horse, but on the return journey the rough-types outside the saloon followed his progress with their surly gazes. They nudged each other and murmured comments and even from some distance away Cassidy heard them uttering his name.

Several of them peeled away from the wall and moved to intercept him, but Cassidy wasn't in the mood to find out what was on their minds and he kept his head down. In short order he mounted up and swung out into the road, but as he passed he looked at the straggling line of men to show he'd noted their interest.

In return he received a measured series of arrogant glares that burned his neck as he left town.

'I've not seen you since you got back,' Deputy Floyd Wright said. 'Everything fine?'

Cassidy broke off from hammering in the latest fence post to face his old deputy.

'I'm settling into my new routine,' he said.

'I'm surprised. You've got the whole town talking. So perhaps your promise to be sheriff again might not be misplaced.'

Cassidy frowned. His desire to regain his star had nothing to do with the townsfolks' view of him. It was a matter of his own self-belief. He was sure he'd been right about Walker's death, except he'd been wrong and that knowledge had dented his confidence.

'I'm pleased I have support,' he said, settling for a neutral response. He considered Floyd's pensive expression. 'But I'd guess those rough-looking types I saw hanging around outside the saloon yesterday are giving you problems.'

Floyd nodded. 'They've been arriving for the last few days. It seems trouble attracts trouble.'

'So things aren't going well between the Matlock and Shaw families, then?'

'Leland's recovering, but despite Benjamin being due back Stanley feels no better about him or Walker. In return, Walker feels the same way about Stanley what with his mother dying in Shaw's hotel.'

Floyd glanced around, frowning, and his pensive posture made Cassidy smile as he remembered how his former deputy usually needed a preamble before he explained what was on his mind.

'But you've not come here to chew the fat, have you?' he prompted.

'No.' Floyd sighed. 'Sheriff Johanson's been looking into Elizabeth Caine's past, so yesterday he went to see Judge Mitchell. He's not come back. I thought you might like to help me track him down.'

Cassidy raised his eyebrows. 'Us two riding off on an investigation again is a bit premature, isn't it?'

'Coming or not?' Floyd said, suppressing a smile with pursed lips.

Cassidy reckoned he didn't need a reason to join his old friend and so ten minutes later the two men rode off.

For the last two years since retiring, Mitchell had lived to the north of town in an isolated house and so they were able to take a route over the river that avoided the town.

They rode in companionable silence. Floyd had relaxed now that Cassidy had agreed to join him and Cassidy found that despite their change in roles he still enjoyed riding with him.

'How is your investigation going?' he asked when Mitchell's house came into view.

93

'Not well,' Floyd said. 'Johanson has so few leads he was thinking about seeing you.'

'I hope the real reason you asked me to come wasn't to save Johanson from having to question me.'

Floyd frowned, but on seeing that Cassidy was smiling he returned a smile.

'I was helping you avoid him.'

Cassidy laughed then looked ahead at the house. Mitchell's abode was a neat timber construction that had been built to last when he had first settled here.

Whenever Cassidy had visited while they'd both been fulfilling their former roles Mitchell had always come out to greet him. But not this time.

They left their horses in the previously empty corral.

'It looks deserted,' Cassidy said with a sigh. 'But Mitchell rarely leaves home these days.'

With Floyd at his side Cassidy headed to the door where he stopped to listen. From inside, he heard creaking and, despite the warmth of the late morning, in the shadows it was cold.

Cassidy backhanded the door open, then stood beside the door. All he could hear was the creaking. He ventured a glance into the darkened interior, then closed his eyes for a moment.

With a sad shake of the head, he drew his gun and raised it beside his cheek then paced inside. Three steps into the house, he halted and consid-

94

ered the terrible scene.

Suspended from the ceiling before the fireplace was Mitchell's body, his charred feet and legs dangling over the cold embers, the blackened bones visible through the patches of torn skin.

'Hellfire,' Floyd said, as he slipped past Cassidy and saw the body.

Cassidy nodded, then set about finding a knife to cut down the body. When with Floyd's help he'd completed the grisly task Cassidy drew a blanket over the tortured form.

For a minute they stood in silent tribute with their heads bowed. Then Cassidy pointed to the door.

'Come on,' he said. 'We need to find out what happened to Johanson.'

Floyd set his hands on his hips, silently noting that Cassidy was no longer in a position to give him orders. Then he moved to the door and opened it but, as he headed outside, a volley of gunfire ripped into the doorframe making him dart back in.

'The men who killed Mitchell presumably,' he said, drawing his gun and standing with his back to the wall.

'How many?' Cassidy asked, joining him.

'Three horses have arrived. Two men are taking cover behind the water trough. Another man is heading around the back.'

'Then we don't let them settle. Cover me.'

This time Floyd didn't complain when Cassidy issued an order. He hurried to the window.

Cassidy stood to the side of the door and gathered his breath to calm himself. He had never thought he'd get to work with Floyd again and strangely he found this predicament preferable to how he'd thought he'd spend his day, hammering in fence posts.

With a smile on his lips he winked at Floyd. His former deputy returned the wink before he smashed out a pane then began firing at a steady rate through the window.

Cassidy counted to five then kicked open the door and charged outside.

A man who had been trying to slip around the back of the house slid to a halt and whirled his gun towards Cassidy, but Cassidy tore off a wild shot then threw himself on his chest. A returned gunshot whistled over his tumbling form as Cassidy rolled and came up on one knee facing the gunman.

He blasted a low shot into the man's guts that bent him double. The man's gun fell from his slack fingers but even before it'd hit the ground, Cassidy had hammered a second slug into his forehead.

The man staggered backwards and crashed into the corral fence, his force being great enough to break through it and tumble him to the ground.

Cassidy turned at the hip to see the gunmen behind the water trough bob up to blast lead at him, but he dived to the ground to lie flat, facing the trough with his gun thrust out.

He ripped a slug into the man on the left that tore a chunk from his chin. The man's head cracked back for him to stand straight before he keeled over on to his back.

The other man moved to dive for cover, but not before Floyd from the house had scythed a shot into his shoulder that spun him around and to the ground.

Cassidy kept his position, waiting for the last attacker to make another foolish move. But when the man stayed down, he glanced at the house to check that Floyd was still covering him.

He jumped to his feet and dashed to the water trough. He stopped five yards from it, his gun poised and waiting for the gunman to risk emerging.

He heard a pained whimper, so he settled his stance.

'You have a way out,' he shouted. 'Come out with your hands high.'

'You'll never take me alive!' the man shouted. He leapt up, his left hand clutching his wounded shoulder, his gun arcing towards Cassidy.

Before he could fire a single shot, Cassidy slammed a slug into his guts, wheeling him backwards for a pace. Then Floyd blasted a volley of lead into his chest that knocked him to his knees, then on to his back.

With a foot raised on the water trough, Cassidy reloaded, listening and looking out for any more surprises. When silence greeted him, he turned to Floyd as he emerged from the house.

'So,' Floyd said with a rueful smile, 'we won't learn anything from these men.'

'Except for one thing.' Cassidy holstered his gun. 'They were amongst the men who were hanging around outside the saloon yesterday.'

Floyd nodded. 'That begs the question of who invited them.'

'This doesn't feel like something Mayor Shaw would organize, so it has to be Walker.' He glanced around. 'But whoever did it, we need to find Johanson.'

Floyd winced. 'After what they did to Mitchell I kind of hope we can't.'

Cassidy limited himself to a frown. Then they checked around the house.

A search of the immediate vicinity didn't reveal the sheriff, or for that matter any sign of him having been here. With Mitchell having been dead for a while, probably even a full day, Cassidy drew Floyd's attention to the tracks.

They scanned the hoofprints made by the dead men's horses intently until they disappeared from view, noting the men had come from town, but a distinct second set of tracks headed towards a distant ridge.

'We'll see where these lead.' Cassidy moved

towards his horse, then stopped. 'Provided you don't mind the two of us acting like we did in the old days.'

'I thought you'd never ask,' Floyd said, smiling for the first time since they'd come to Mitchell's house.

'Please don't hurt me,' Sheriff Edwin Johanson whined.

Rockwell Trent watched Johanson struggle against the bonds with which he'd secured him to the discarded wagon wheel, but he found no give in the firm knots.

Rockwell turned and paced away to stand on the edge of the rocky promontory where he could peer down at the plains below.

'We're ten miles out of Monotony,' he said, then swirled round to glare at Johanson. He raised his eyebrows. 'But if you don't tell me who killed Elizabeth Caine, your screams will make the towns-folk's blood run cold.'

Rockwell stalked towards Johanson. He cracked his knuckles then loomed over him. His shadow fell across Johanson's face as he drew his gun and held it up to the light.

'I don't know. I don't—' Johanson lowered his head. 'But let me go and I'll find the killer.'

Rockwell hunkered down beside Johanson and grabbed his chin. Johanson squirmed and tried to wrest himself away, but Rockwell gathered a firm grip and raised his face so he could peer into his eyes.

'It doesn't work like that. Talk now or die.'

Johanson firmed his jaw with a rare show of defiance.

'Then you'll have to kill me.'

'It doesn't work like that either. I intend to find out how much pain you can withstand and yet still hang on to your worthless existence. Judge Mitchell looked like he suffered plenty, but that'll be nothing compared to your suffering.'

Rockwell drew Johanson's head down so that he looked at his gun. Then slowly he aimed the weapon at Johanson's bound right hand.

'What . . . what you going to do?'

'I'm going to ask my question. If you don't answer, I shoot off a finger. Then I'll ask the same question.' Rockwell released Johanson's chin then one by one he drew his fingers down to bunch them into a fist. 'I reckon you'll answer before I start looking for other bits to blast off.'

Johanson tugged hard on his bonds but his hand only shifted an inch. He clawed the fingers into a tight fist, but Rockwell grabbed Johanson's hand and prised open the fingers then aimed his gun down at the index finger.

'I can't, I can't,' Johanson babbled. 'I don't know who killed her. Tell me why you think I do know because I don't know what you mean. I just don't know what—'

Johanson uttered a sob and that first admittance that he no longer cared about keeping his dignity opened him up to a tide of remorse.

He wailed. Tears cascaded down his face. His mouth contorted into desperate shapes as he gibbered and begged for his life.

Rockwell watched his bout of pleading, keeping his face impassive and not letting the disgust he felt register. Only when Johanson slumped, his head falling to lie on his chest, did Rockwell move.

He placed a hand beneath Johanson's chin, raised his head, and gave him a comforting smile that made hope spring up in Johanson's eyes. Then he raised his gun an inch and roved it in decreasing circles to home in on the finger.

He stopped with the gun resting against the skin.

'Now talk,' he whispered.

'I can't. But . . . but . . . but I do have a proposition.' Johanson took a deep breath. 'Whatever you've been paid to kill me, I'll double it for you to kill whoever hired you.'

Rockwell rubbed his chin, then stood and backed away for a pace.

'I have a deal and there's one thing you need to know about me: I honour my deals.'

'But from what I've heard about you, you only kill for money and that means you're open to a better offer.'

Rockwell glanced at Johanson's right hand.

101

'You may be right. You have five seconds, then I start firing.'

Johanson closed his eyes, breathing deeply.

'I'll pay you five hundred dollars,' he blurted.

Rockwell snorted and cocked his gun. 'You're not even close.'

'A thousand, then.' Johanson watched Rockwell aim the gun at his hand. 'Two . . . three thousand!'

Rockwell kept the gun aimed, but then he raised it and turned his gaze on Johanson.

'Seems you can talk sense when you're moti-vated.' Rockwell leaned down. 'But how would a lawman get his hands on so much money?'

Johanson gulped. 'What does that matter?'

'It matters plenty. Something's wrong in this town and I'm being paid to sniff it out. Talk about where you got the money and that might save your life.'

'That's not got nothing to do with Elizabeth,' Johanson whined with a resigned expression. A moment later he jerked backwards against the wheel, his head lolling as blood flew.

A moment later the distant crack of gunfire sounded.

Rockwell stared at the body, seeing the raw wound between Johanson's eyes, his own trade-mark method of dispatch taunting him.

'Again,' he murmured, despair rooting him to the spot.

Within moments anger won through and he

102

swirled round. Nobody was to be seen close by, but when he surveyed the plains in search of his tormentor a thin smile broke his grim visage.

A rider was heading away towards Riker's Bend.

CHAPTER 9

When Cassidy first saw movement ahead it came from the rise at Riker's Bend.

Cassidy dismissed the location as a coincidence so that he could concentrate on the task in hand and with Floyd at his side he moved on. Closer to, he saw that a man was making his way around the river side of the rise.

They had halved the distance to him when he disappeared from view. In those last moments Cassidy saw that he was black-clad, and that he was probably Rockwell Trent. The determined way that he was looking ahead made Cassidy think that he was tracking someone.

They hurried on to the rise. After a brief debate they dismounted and split up, aiming to outflank him. While Floyd followed Rockwell around the rise Cassidy climbed to the top.

When he peered over the top he couldn't see where Rockwell had gone. But 150 yards ahead and below him, Zachary McKinney was standing beside the river watering his horse with his back to him.

Cassidy hadn't seen him since they'd returned to town, but he presumed that Zachary's gloomy forecast had proved correct and the arrival of Rockwell as Walker's protector had meant his services were no longer required.

Cassidy took a deep breath to calm himself and to avoid dwelling on the similarities the situation had with last year's incident. He picked out a route that would use the available cover and avoid Zachary seeing him, then scurried to the nearest boulder, then to the next.

When he reached ground level he had halved the distance to him and even better he could now see where Rockwell had gone to ground. He had hunkered down behind a squat boulder and was peering over it at Zachary.

Cassidy settled in his position and awaited developments.

Within a minute, Zachary led his horse back from the river. As he moved to mount up, Rockwell with a determined motion levered his long legs out and stood, a rifle swinging to his shoulder.

'Stop!' Cassidy shouted, stepping out from behind his covering rock. 'This is Cassidy Yates and you're putting those hands high.'

Rockwell flinched, then turned and let his rifle swing loose to point downwards.

'You've made a big mistake,' he muttered, raising his left hand to chest level. 'No man sneaks up on the Iceman and lives.'

'From what I'd heard, nobody ever sneaked up on you in the first place. Perhaps the Iceman is slipping.'

Rockwell's right eye twitched, acknowledging that Cassidy had been right that he wasn't as confident about his abilities as he made out. Cassidy gestured at him to drop his gun.

Rockwell laid his rifle at his feet, never taking his eyes off him. Then to Cassidy's directions he unhooked his gunbelt and dropped it to the side.

Cassidy looked up, but it was to see that Zachary had used the distraction to mount up. Within moments he'd spurred his horse on to a gallop. Cassidy shouted at him to stop, but he didn't heed the warning.

He shouted again, but the sound died on his lips. Something about Zachary's posture as he rode away tapped at a memory he couldn't quite recall. He was still trying to form the memory when Floyd hurried into view.

Cassidy beckoned him to pursue Zachary. Then he faced Rockwell.

'Why were you following Zachary?' he asked. 'And what do you know about Judge Mitchell's demise?'

'I'm saying nothing,' Rockwell said. 'But know this: you've got the wrong man.'

Cassidy shrugged. 'I didn't think you were the kind of man who'd beg for clemency.'

'I'm not begging,' Rockwell said, smirking and regaining his usual composure. 'I just want you to know it'd have been easier on you if you'd let me finish what I'd started.'

When the cortège reached town the sight ahead made Cassidy come to a sudden halt. He glanced at Floyd and frowned. Then they both carried on down the road.

They had already been in a sombre frame of mind after Floyd's pursuit of Zachary McKinney had failed and with the bodies of Judge Mitchell and, after making another grim discovery, Sheriff Johanson trailing behind them strung over horses. Now the banners that were being stretched across the road yesterday were in place and they all proclaimed the news that Monotony welcomed Benjamin Shaw home.

The presence of the happy crowd gathered around the podium outside the hotel suggested that arrival was imminent.

'I'll let you deal with the rest of this,' Cassidy said. 'Nobody wants me around while this celebration's going on.'

'Only a few in town are against you,' Floyd said. 'Remember that.'

Cassidy opened his mouth aiming to ask him to name one person other than himself who actively supported him, but a loud cheer stopped him from speaking.

He looked to the hotel and through the bustling crowd he saw a person he didn't recognize for a moment climb up on to the podium. This man raised his arms for quiet, but that only made everyone cheer even louder. Hats flew in the air, marching music started up from somewhere, and the cheering went on.

Only when Cassidy got closer did he confirm who the man was. The last year had changed Benjamin Shaw. He was now thick-set and stooped, all sign of his former youthful nature gone.

Floyd glanced at Cassidy silently conveying his surprise in how much Benjamin had changed then veered away to the sheriff's office with Rockwell. He left the bodies outside and as Cassidy had seen the undertaker amongst the crowd he stayed with them.

Patiently he waited for him to show his usual ability to sniff out work and come over, but the people on the edge of the crowd saw the bodies first.

Several men drifted over and so Cassidy dismounted and backed away to let them see who had died. Their shocked cries gathered more attention and so the periphery of the crowd gradually peeled away to form a new huddle.

The commotion caught the attention of the people closer to the podium and then finally the people on the podium. Both Benjamin Shaw and his father looked at the horses, then at Cassidy.

Cassidy had wished to avoid meeting Benjamin for as long as possible, but he figured he couldn't delay the first encounter now and so he set off. Before him the crowd parted then filled in behind so that by the time he reached the podium a solid wall of people circled him.

While Benjamin came down the steps, Cassidy couldn't help but notice that many of the surrounding people were the rough types who'd arrived recently, and they were all smirking. Then for the first time in a year Cassidy faced the man he had wrongly identified as a killer.

Silence descended on the crowd, although shocked murmuring still came from those who were outside the sheriff's office.

Cassidy stepped up to Benjamin. He considered him, noting his drawn face, the flecks of white hair that he shouldn't have acquired for many years, the bruises that marred his face.

'I was wrong,' Cassidy said in a voice that was loud enough to be heard by everyone who had gathered. 'I thought you'd killed Walker Matlock, but when I tracked down Walker a week ago, I accepted my mistake. For the wrong I did you, I apologize.'

Sharp intakes of breath sounded from many in the crowd and Cassidy was pleased to hear several people murmur in a supportive way, but the declaration did nothing to lighten Benjamin's grim expression.

Benjamin looked him up and down. His eyes narrowed. His face reddened. His mouth opened and closed but no words emerged. Then he advanced a long pace and launched a swinging punch at Cassidy's jaw that sent him reeling to the ground.

Cassidy had seen the punch coming, but he didn't try to avoid it and he even exaggerated his fall so that he rolled and came to rest against the boots of the watching crowd. They backed away, letting him get to his feet.

Cassidy took his time, but as he straightened he received a flailing punch to the cheek. He avoided falling by stumbling backward for a pace. But staying on his feet only let him receive a short-armed jab to the guts that made him drop to his knees and a backhanded slap to the face that sent him spinning to the ground.

He rolled several times, this time without exaggerating his plight, and when he came to rest he took a moment to compose himself.

He was determined to take the advice he'd given last year of letting this confrontation play itself out to avoid the resentment festering on. Even so he was relieved when he got to his feet and found that Stanley had stepped forward. Stanley placed a hand on his son's shoulder and whispered calm words.

Although at first Benjamin maintained the stern set of his jaw, slowly he relaxed and nodded. He came over to stand before Cassidy. He still stood truculently, but he kept his fists lowered.

'A lousy, stinking year in jail for something I didn't do,' he said.

Cassidy shrugged. 'Some might say that was a fair punishment for wounding a man.'

Benjamin's eyes flared and he advanced on Cassidy, forcing Stanley to hurry on and grab his shoulders.

'You apologized, but it meant nothing,' Benjamin roared, 'because you can't accept you were wrong about everything that night. I didn't shoot anyone.'

Cassidy searched for the right words to say, already regretting his previous comment.

'If that's true, then what you went through must have been rough on you.'

'It sure was. A year of hard labour, the beatings, the other prisoners. . . .'

He cast a glance at the surrounding crowd and although he received numerous supportive murmured comments, some of the fight left his eyes and he lowered his head, showing a hint of the man he had been. He turned away, shrugged his father's hands from his shoulders, and walked past the podium and through the people to the hotel.

With the confrontation over, the crowd dispersed to wander over to the sheriff's office,

111

leaving Cassidy standing alone. Cassidy waited until the circle had cleared then looked down the road and saw that outside Leland Matlock's house Walker and Millicent were watching proceedings.

The moment they saw him looking at them they returned to the house, although Walker dallied to cast a significant glance at the hotel where Benjamin was disappearing from view.

Cassidy batted the dust from his knees and flexed his jaw, finding he'd got through his beating with only a few sore spots. When he was ready to head back to his horse he found that Stanley was returning from his consideration of the bodies.

'Don't blame Benjamin,' he said.

'I don't,' Cassidy said. 'I deserved that.'

'You did, but nothing else. The matter's now over. I'll see to that.'

Last year Leland Matlock had provided the same promise, but even if that had turned out to be misplaced, he nodded.

'Obliged.'

Stanley glanced over his shoulder at the milling crowd and then at the bodies outside the sheriff's office.

'But it'd appear that other matters may be starting.'

'They are, but I have every confidence that Deputy Wright will be able to work out who killed Elizabeth Caine and now Judge Mitchell and Sheriff Johanson.'

112

'Floyd's a good man, but he's a follower not a leader. I need a proper sheriff to get to the bottom of this.'

Cassidy opened his mouth, but then he closed it with his thoughts left unsaid. He would never be able to convince Stanley that he was the right man for the job.

'I wish you luck with your search.'

Cassidy moved to leave, but Stanley stepped to the side to block his way.

'I don't need to search far.' He removed a star from his pocket, an emblem of office that until a few minutes ago had graced the unworthy form of Sheriff Johanson. He held it out. 'Now is the time to put the past behind us and move on.'

Cassidy stared at the star, still presuming that despite Stanley's comments this was an elaborate insult designed to knock him down.

'Me?' he murmured.

'Sure,' Stanley said. 'If you want the job, you can once again be our sheriff.'

CHAPTER 10

Cassidy walked into the sheriff's office to find that Rockwell Trent had now been locked in a cell and Deputy Wright was writing out a summary of the recent events. Floyd looked up and smiled.

'Crowd still not moving on?' he asked.

'The deaths shocked them,' Cassidy said. 'They don't want to go back to their business yet and that was before they heard the news.'

'What news?'

Cassidy removed the star from his pocket. The sight surprised Floyd as much as it had surprised Cassidy. His eyes opened even wider when Cassidy pinned the star on his jacket.

'I'm the new sheriff,' he said simply.

Floyd searched Cassidy's eyes, his lips curling with a smile as he waited for him to confirm he was joking.

'Does Stanley know?'

'He appointed me.'

Floyd came out from behind his desk, still looking bemused.

'Then I congratulate you,' he said cautiously, holding out a hand.

Cassidy shook his hand. 'Perhaps you should save the congratulations. The only reason I can think of for the reappointment after he's refused to talk to me for a year is he doesn't expect me to survive until sundown.'

'With Benjamin and Walker back in town, he might be right.' Floyd tipped back his hat. 'We'll make sure that doesn't happen.'

Cassidy nodded then turned to the cells to consider his prisoner.

'So, Rockwell,' he said, raising his voice, 'are you ready to talk?'

Rockwell raised his head slowly to consider Cassidy, but his cold eyes registered no hint of concern about his predicament. He rolled his legs on to his cot and leaned back against the side bars.

'Nope.'

'You're a hired gun, so I'm more interested in the man who hired you. Tell me what Walker told you to do and I'll release you.' When Rockwell said nothing Cassidy walked back and forth three times, tapping his fist against his thigh. When he stopped he leaned on the bars and peered at Rockwell through a gap. 'Then try this: if you're innocent, I need to find the guilty man before he kills again.'

Rockwell shook his head and swung his legs to the floor. Slowly he stood.

'You're a good man. So take my advice and stop investigating. You're fighting to protect someone who isn't worth it.'

'Is that Walker?' Cassidy waited for an answer but Rockwell remained silent. 'Then Zachary McKinney?'

Rockwell grabbed a bar in each hand and peered at Cassidy through a gap.

'Give up,' he whispered, 'or you'll be the next to die.'

'Two weeks ago I promised you we'd talk,' Leland Matlock said, peering at Cassidy around the side of the door. 'And now we can.'

'I'm pleased you're walking,' Cassidy said, although he noted that Leland moved with difficulty and his sallow complexion said he was far from well. 'But events might have invalidated what you had to say.'

Leland stood back to let him enter then bade him to follow him into the living-room.

'Elizabeth's return wasn't the only matter I wanted to talk to you about.'

While Cassidy watched Leland edge himself gingerly into a chair, he wondered if he should risk jeopardizing this move towards reconciliation with the news that Leland probably hadn't heard. But Leland was a proud man and he wouldn't accept duplicity. So when Leland looked up he held his jacket out to show him his star.

'You'd only speak to me when I was no longer sheriff. But Edwin Johanson was killed earlier today. Stanley Shaw reappointed me.'

Leland took this information with barely a change to his blank expression.

'That's an odd way for him to annoy me.' He watched Cassidy smile as he added this explanation to the growing list of theories for his unexpected and quick reappointment. 'But that doesn't change my opinion about you. Walker's back and that's more than I could have hoped for.'

'Except Walker and Benjamin are angry. This could end in bloodshed, so the mistakes made last time must be avoided this time.'

'They have unresolved business, so this time you need to do the right thing and watch Benjamin.'

'When I said mistakes, I didn't mean mine.'

Leland narrowed his eyes. 'Don't ruin our new start by blaming Walker for Benjamin's actions.'

'I wasn't. I was looking at you.'

Leland shrugged. 'My ability to control Walker is as poor as Stanley's ability to control Benjamin.'

'I know. They're grown men who've suffered.' Cassidy took a steady pace forward. 'Just like you and Stanley have.'

'What you getting at, Cassidy?'

'When the town founder and the town mayor won't speak to each other, it creates tension. When

117

the town founder's wife dies in the mayor's hotel and the sons are at loggerheads, that tension is set to boil over. The best way to relieve the tension is for you and Stanley to resolve your differences.'

Leland opened and closed his mouth soundlessly, lost for words. Before he could find his voice footfalls sounded in the hall followed by the arrival of Walker and Millicent, who both glared at him with contempt.

'Why are you annoying my father?' Walker demanded.

'This isn't a social call,' Cassidy said. He held out his jacket to let Walker see his star. The sight made Walker raise his eyebrows in the same way that everyone he'd passed on the boardwalk had. 'Edwin Johanson was killed today. Rockwell Trent's in a cell as my main suspect.'

Walker took this information with barely a flicker of concern.

'Anyone who crosses me is making a bad mistake. Free him.'

'Did Judge Mitchell make a bad mistake?' Cassidy waited for Walker to reply, but he said nothing. 'Three dead men are at his house, men who someone hired to come after me. If I can link them to you, you'll be in the cell next to Rockwell's.'

'Stop accusing my son,' Leland said, 'and do your duty.'

Walker grunted that he agreed then turned to

118

the door.

'One other thing.' Cassidy waited until Walker stopped. He lowered his voice to a supportive tone. 'Benjamin's back and he's angry, but it doesn't have to end the way it ended the last time. Apparently he's in the Silver Streak mouthing off about you. So stay away and let him calm down.'

Walker muttered something to himself then left. A few moments later the outside door slammed shut.

The remaining people stood silently until Leland levered himself out of his chair and faced him.

'You failed Walker before,' he said. 'Don't side with Benjamin again.'

Before Cassidy could retort he turned to the door. Millicent moved to help him walk, but he shot her a stern look that made her stay back. She watched him until he left the room then swirled round to face Cassidy.

While Leland's receding footfalls sounded, she ground her jaw, suggesting she was considering then rejecting various things to say. At last she spoke, although she couldn't look him in the eye.

'Thank you for bringing Walker back,' she said simply. She turned to leave.

'I wish you well,' Cassidy said, following her into the hall. 'I hope your second chance with Walker works out.'

She gulped. 'I can't forgive you for the last year,

119

but swallowing your pride and admitting you were wrong must have been hard.'

He went past her to the front door where he stopped. He watched her move away down the hall and he almost let them part on a good note of partial reconciliation. But his confidence was growing with every moment he became used to the star on his chest and so he coughed, halting her.

'I've always been sure about what I saw that night last year, but now it seems that Walker didn't die and Benjamin claims he didn't even shoot him.'

'I wouldn't believe anything Benjamin says.'

'I don't any more, so answer me one question: has Walker got a gunshot wound on his chest?'

She swirled round to face him, her eyes flaring with a mixture of anger and surprise. Then she turned and headed off down the hall.

When Cassidy left the house he was unsure if that meeting had gone well or badly.

As he made his way back to the law office he saw Walker storming into the saloon. In irritation he gripped his hands into fists and hurried down the boardwalk.

He reached the saloon a couple of minutes after Walker had gone inside. Benjamin was drinking at a corner table. Walker had his back to him while he stood hunched over at the bar.

Cassidy noted the similarities to the situation in this saloon last year.

As the two hotheads were now in the same place he was minded to drag them into the centre of the room and knock their heads together until they agreed to take their disagreement no further. Then he noticed who was sitting with Benjamin.

Around him were ten men, all rough-clad and all were amongst the men who'd been loitering outside the saloon the day before. He went over to stand before Benjamin, who saw him coming and with his colleagues he looked at him sneering.

'What you want with me, lawman?' he asked.

'I'm interested in your new friends,' Cassidy said. 'They were skulking around town yesterday, but not all of them are here now.'

Benjamin looked at the nearest man, who shrugged.

'I don't know where they went,' this man said.

'I do,' Cassidy said. 'They went to Judge Mitchell's house.'

'You can't blame his death on them.'

'Perhaps not, but as they're full of lead now that don't matter none.' Cassidy waited until the various sneering expressions tightened. 'Any of you step out of line, you'll get the same treatment.'

Cassidy gave them all a significant look then backed away for a pace. He had aimed to leave the saloon then, but a slow handclap sounded. Cassidy turned to see that Walker was leaning back against the bar while clapping his hands together with an insistent rhythm.

'Obliged,' Walker said. 'I've waited a long time for you to stand up to Benjamin Shaw.'

'Cassidy would never help me,' Benjamin said, scraping back his chair and standing. 'He's always sided with you.'

Cassidy raised two hands as Walker moved from the bar with a sharp retort on his lips.

'I'm not on anyone's side but the law's,' Cassidy said. 'Stanley Shaw appointed me sheriff and Leland Matlock told me to keep the peace. If those two men trust me, their sons can too.'

The two men glared past Cassidy at each other, but Cassidy's warning made it hard for them to find an opening to continue arguing.

With mutual snorts of derision Walker turned to the door and Benjamin sat back down.

Cassidy waited until Walker had left then followed him out. He was pleased to see that Walker was heading back to his house. He had no doubt that a showdown between these men was likely, but it would be inevitable only if he couldn't resolve who was behind the recent spree of murders.

He moved to head across the road to the hotel aiming to give Stanley the same talk as he'd given Leland – that he needed to reconcile with Walker to reduce the tension. He'd taken only a few paces when movement to his side caught his attention.

He turned, then flinched back in surprise when Millicent emerged from the shadows. She kept her head bowed and she fidgeted and coughed before she spoke.

'The answer's no,' she murmured.

Cassidy pondered, then provided an apologetic shrug.

'Obliged for the answer. What was the question?'

She patted her ribs. 'Walker doesn't have a scar.'

Cassidy glanced away rubbing his jaw. His question had been a speculative one with no expectation that this would be the answer and so where this information led him he didn't know.

'I'm obliged for your trust. That revelation must have been hard for you to make.'

'That's my concern,' she snapped. Then she got control of herself with a shake. 'You needed to know. I heard what was said in there and Benjamin will overreact if he finds out that Walker wasn't injured in the first place. So I hope you'll put aside your personal feelings and protect Walker.'

'Of course, but right now the only people not wanting protection are Benjamin and Walker themselves.'

'I know.' She sighed and looked away. 'And there's other things you don't know about.'

Cassidy waited for her to say more, then moved closer.

'Such as?'

'It's. . . .' She rocked from foot to foot then looked up and down the road nervously, as if someone might be watching them. 'We'll talk, but not here. You remember the place down by the river where we used to go?'

'How could I forget Riker's Bend?' he said.

Something about his lower tone made her look him in the eye and smile for the first time.

'I didn't mean it that way. I was thinking about the good times we once enjoyed there. Meet me there in an hour and I'll tell you about Zachary McKinney.'

CHAPTER 11

As Cassidy rode out of town towards the spot where he and Millicent used to picnic, but which he'd never thought he'd remember fondly again, he rode tall in the saddle. He felt as if his recent problems had fallen away.

He wasn't fooling himself that Millicent's worried request to see him might herald them being able to accept each other again, and neither was he making light of the tension in town. He had several murders to solve and a potential showdown was imminent between Monotony's two most important families.

But now that he'd regained his star, these felt as though they were solvable problems.

When he'd ridden past the rise he looked around to see if she'd arrived first, but he couldn't see her. So he dismounted and walked his horse to the river, then tethered it and walked back and forth, letting himself remember the good times he'd enjoyed here.

He even sat on the boulder where Benjamin had sat and had thrown stones into the water. The action further helped to exorcise the bad memories this place gave him.

When he judged that an hour had passed since she'd asked him to come here, he continued to wait patiently whiling away a pleasant afternoon.

Presently approaching hoofbeats broke his reverie. Even though the noise was too loud to be a single rider he turned with a smile on his lips, hoping to see Millicent, but instead a line of ten riders was galloping around the rise towards him.

He backed away to his horse while watching them and as they drew closer to he saw they were the men who had been with Benjamin in the saloon. Worse, most of them had drawn guns and they all had determined postures.

He moved to mount up as the leading man drew his gun and blasted lead at him. The slug whistled by some feet over his head, suggesting it had been a warning shot, but Cassidy still resolved not to wait around and find out what they wanted.

He rolled into the saddle keeping low and swung his horse around and then with a shake of the reins he moved off. Another slug whined by, this time no closer than the previous one had been. This at least let Cassidy decide that they weren't planning to kill him.

Within fifty yards he had speeded to a gallop and was heading back around the other side of the rise towards Monotony, some four miles on. He concentrated on fast riding, leaning forward in the saddle and not risking slowing down by looking back to see how close they were.

More gunshots whistled by, all wild. Cassidy gritted his teeth avoiding letting them goad him into returning fire and so taking his mind off the task of reaching town as quickly as possible.

For several minutes he rode on until hoofbeats thundered behind him and then around him as with his peripheral vision he saw men spreading out to outflank him.

Then they moved in. Cassidy ignored them as he stared ahead at the town, now less than two miles on, the individual buildings becoming visible.

A sharp pain cut across Cassidy's shoulders, the shock so sudden Cassidy wondered what had happened. He looked down and saw the rope resting on his upper arms and realized one of his pursuers had lassoed him.

He released a hand from the reins aiming to prise the rope off, but he was too late.

The rope pulled back tightening across his chest and dragging both hands from the reins. He sat upright swaying as he tried to balance on his runaway horse while clawing at the rope that was biting into his chest. He managed to grip the rope and slide it upwards, but then he was dragged backwards as his captor slowed his horse and drew him in.

127

He struggled, keeping himself mounted as his captor pulled back, but then the strain became too much and he flew out of the saddle.

With his arms waving he became airborne for several seconds before he crashed to the ground on his back, the shock blasting the air from his lungs and making him think he'd shattered every bone in his body.

Worse was to come when he slid to a halt and after a moment of stillness his hurrying captor sped past him and tugged him on.

The men whooped with delight and Cassidy could do nothing to stop himself being dragged along the ground, the friction burning his back. Then mercifully he came to rest but he still felt too jarred to do anything but look upwards as the riders gathered to look down at him.

Several men dismounted and stood around him. Cassidy bided his time, flexing his muscles and confirming that he hadn't broken anything. Presently the rope tightened and his captor leaned over him, aiming to drag him upright.

Cassidy swung up to a sitting position and aimed a bunched fist at the man's face, but he'd overestimated his recovery. He managed to raise himself for only a foot and his punch wafted by several feet short.

His futile attempt to fight back made the man laugh and then with a few sharp gestures he ordered others to secure him.

This time Cassidy saved his energies. In short order they trussed him up, dragged him to his horse, and secured him over the back. Then they led him away.

Throughout the operation nobody had spoken leaving Cassidy to surmise as to why they wanted him. He didn't reach any firm conclusions, but he reckoned that if they were following Benjamin's instructions, he would get confirmation soon enough, and the answer was unlikely to be a pleasant one.

They headed away from town, going back along the riverside and even upside-down Cassidy worked out that they were taking him to Judge Mitchell's old house. When they arrived he was tipped off the horse and pulled to his feet.

Cassidy was pleased to find that when he'd been stood up he was able to stand unaided. But in order to maintain the illusion he was too weak to fight back he let his shoulders slump and he staggered when he tried to move.

The men holding his ropes kept him upright and then with his feet dragging they took him to the door. Cassidy kept his head bowed until Benjamin Shaw spoke up.

'You did well,' he said.

Cassidy threatened. 'If you've harmed her, I'll—'

'Be quiet,' Benjamin snapped. In five long paces he stepped up to him and delivered a stinging slap to his cheek that cracked his head to the side. The men holding him needed to keep a firm grip to keep him upright.

Cassidy flexed his jaw then looked at Benjamin. 'The threat stands.'

Benjamin narrowed his eyes, his fists bunching, but then the man who had lassoed Cassidy spoke up.

'If he's talking about Millicent,' he said, 'she never showed for their meeting.'

'Does that satisfy you?' Benjamin asked. He waited for Cassidy to nod. 'My problem is with you and Walker only. You both made me fester away in jail for something I never did. So now you get to suffer.'

'I'm the sheriff again, Benjamin. If you treat me like you treated Mitchell, you'll fester away for a lot longer than a year.'

Benjamin gestured at the men who had now all come inside.

'These are the friends I made in prison. They're eager to start fighting back, but what happened to Mitchell had nothing to do with us. Those men took out their anger on a judge, any judge.'

'I believe you, but I wouldn't expect you to thirst after revenge. You were a decent man and your father deserves to get that man back.'

Benjamin sneered then gestured. The two men holding Cassidy pushed him forward.

They walked him across the room and into a back room. At the end of this room was a door leading down into the dugout Mitchell had built when he'd first settled here.

One man opened the door and then they pushed him down into the dugout.

Cassidy hadn't been in the room before and he had but a moment to look around and see that Mitchell had used the area as a storeroom. Then Benjamin blocked the door.

'I'm leaving to kill Walker,' he said. Benjamin backed away for a pace. 'While you wait you can comfort yourself with the thought that if he kills me, I won't come back and you'll rot in there.'

Benjamin slammed the door and plunged Cassidy into darkness.

Millicent Matlock was swinging a wicker basket when she came into the sheriff's office.

Rockwell watched her approach the deputy, noting that his actions were the same as they had been when the last visitor had entered.

Since he'd been locked in the cell he'd studied Floyd's routine. He now understood his behaviour and if he got a chance to escape, he would use that knowledge, but until that moment came he had bided his time and brooded.

Of all the disasters that had befallen him recently his current predicament was the worst, as just when he'd worked out who had been tormenting him, he faced failure. Unless he escaped, he couldn't defend Walker against the hired guns

Benjamin had amassed and who he'd only been able to watch through the grill window when they left town.

So he watched Millicent in case she had a message for him, but she ignored him as she sat on the edge of Floyd's desk and chatted about how happy she was that Walker was back.

'I'm pleased life might get back to normal,' Floyd said.

'Me too, so could you give Cassidy a message?' She waited until Floyd nodded. 'I said I'd meet him by the river, but I got delayed and I couldn't go. He'll be awfully mad with me, so please tell him I'm sorry.'

'Sure,' Floyd said. He leaned back in his chair, his raised eyebrows registering his surprise.

'Don't look shocked. We talked and made peace. I don't want a misunderstanding to reopen the wounds.' She turned to leave, then stopped and flinched, as if she'd remembered something. She turned back and placed the basket on the desk. 'I forgot I'd brought the fruitcake I baked for Walker to celebrate his homecoming. I'd like my friends to have a piece.'

She withdrew two large chunks and placed them on the desk.

'That sure looks appetizing,' Floyd said, eyeing the cake. He took a bite then chewed and nodded enthusiastically. 'I reckon Cassidy's piece could be a good deal smaller when he returns.'

132

'I'll check with him and it'd better not be.' She waggled a finger at the deputy then laughed and left the office.

She didn't look in Rockwell's direction, leaving him to sigh and draw his legs up on his cot. Floyd heard the sigh and he came over to the cell while still eating the cake.

'Sigh all you want,' he said, 'but you're not getting a piece.'

Rockwell merely scowled at the deputy. Floyd stood awhile chewing, but when he confirmed that Rockwell was ignoring him he moved to pop in the last piece of cake. Then he stumbled.

He threw out a hand to grab hold of something but the hand closed on air and so he toppled over to land on his side where he uttered a long groan, then stilled.

Rockwell jumped to his feet and hurried to the bars. Floyd was breathing shallowly and he appeared to be unconscious.

Rockwell knelt and thrust an arm through the bars reaching for the body, but the deputy had fallen several feet from the cell. Even at the extent of his reach he could only brush the sole of Floyd's boot. He put that disappointment from his mind and thought quickly about how he could use this unexpected opportunity.

To his dismay the door opened, but the person who entered was Millicent.

'I took pity on you,' she said breezily. 'I bought

you another—'

Her gaze darted around the office until it fell on Floyd's fallen body. She appraised him then looked up at Rockwell, smiling.

'Will he be fine?' Rockwell said.

'He will be.' She placed the basket on the floor then slipped the uneaten piece of cake inside. 'But I won't be needing the second piece.'

Rockwell nodded. 'Don't stand around congratulating yourself. Get me out of here.'

Three minutes later she was at the door looking outside while Rockwell stayed behind her, now armed. Floyd was locked in Rockwell's cell, bound and gagged for when he came to.

The sun had set and in the lowering light few people were about. She pointed upstairs at the storeroom above the sheriff's office and without question Rockwell nodded then followed her down the boardwalk.

At the door she produced a key then quickly entered and led him up the narrow stairs until they emerged into a room above the law office. Here crates and boxes had been stacked in an untidy tangle and after negotiating a route to the window, Rockwell could look down at the road through a dusty window that faced the hotel across the road.

'Is the showdown imminent?'

'Probably,' she said at his shoulder. 'Benjamin's been acting oddly and Walker says it'll be tonight or never.'

'For Benjamin it'll be never.'

She nodded then backed away for a pace.

Something about her silent withdrawal made Rockwell turn, his movement coming at the same time as he heard a noise. He jerked towards the sound, but he was already too late.

From the darkness a hand slapped down on his holster and a gun barrel poked into the small of his back.

'You're wrong,' the gruff voice of Zachary McKinney whispered in his ear. 'For you it's always been never.'

CHAPTER 12

The sliver of light cast beneath the bottom of the door was growing dim and on the other side of the door his captors' low murmuring was sounding for the first time in hours.

Cassidy had worked out that two men had stayed to guard him while Benjamin and the rest had returned to town.

Using the limited light he again explored his small prison, but the door was the only way out and aside from two empty crates by the side wall there was nothing inside. He kicked one crate as he passed and it creaked. So experimentally he shook the top and found that the planks were loose.

Working quietly he prised away a short plank. Then with his makeshift weapon held low and providing some comfort he resumed his pacing.

Through the door he heard occasional words and he guessed his captors were debating what was happening in Monotony. Then a low and mocking bout of sniggering sounded and the two men approached the door.

'Want anything?' one man asked, his sneering tone suggesting that he had a retort in mind no matter what Cassidy said.

Cassidy was about to say that he did, figuring that getting them to open the door would be his only chance to escape. But talking to them was probably the least likely way he might succeed, so he kept quiet.

Muttering sounded then the guard banged on the door.

'Wake up in there!' he demanded.

Cassidy stayed still and he even breathed quietly through his mouth.

Another demand for him to reply sounded. Then silence reigned for several seconds.

'What's he doing, Brady?'

'Perhaps he's escaped.'

'There's no way out.'

'But he's been to this house before. Perhaps he found a way to—'

'He's no gopher.'

The argument raged and with mounting hope Cassidy willed them to worry themselves into coming to investigate. Slowly he paced to the wall and slipped down behind the crates to await developments.

The muttering ended and then the door rattled and swung open, increasing the light level.

'Stay here, Jack,' the nearest guard said. 'I'll investigate.'

'All right, but give me your gun in case it's a trick.'

Rattling sounded. Then a brand flooded the small room with light.

Brady's cautious footfalls approached the crate. The brand lit the wall above the crate, the edge of that light lowering.

Crouched down Cassidy clutched his short plank and waited. A moment before the approaching light reached his body he leapt to his feet and with a long sweep of his arm he slapped the plank against Brady's head. It broke over his chin and the swipe was strong enough to make him stumble.

As Brady righted himself then moved to swing the brand at him Cassidy barged his way between the crates then grabbed his arm and thrust the burning brand he was carrying into his face.

A screech echoed in the small room as Brady fell backwards clawing at his face and trying to bat away the burning embers. Before he could recover Cassidy was on him.

He grabbed his collar, raised him from the floor, and threw him against the wall, then again. On the third push, Brady's head cracked against the wall with a dull thud. He slumped.

A glance at Brady's holster confirmed he didn't have a gun. Then Cassidy turned to the door. From his angle he could see only a few feet beyond the door and the other guard Jack was cautiously staying back. If he were to lock the door, Cassidy would lose the progress he'd made.

'What's happening?' Jack asked, his voice coming from several yards beyond the door.

Moving silently Cassidy moved to the side of the door and put a hand to it, getting a firm grip while keeping his hand out of view.

'Are you all right, Brady?' Jack persisted.

Cassidy stayed still and after asking his question again Jack shuffled closer to the door. His shadow fell across the rectangle of light cast through the open doorway. He raised an arm to grab hold of the door.

Cassidy waited until the hand reached around the end of the door aiming to drag it shut. Then he leapt forward, putting his weight behind the door and slamming it into Jack's body.

A pained grunt sounded and Cassidy managed only to half-shut the door, so he pulled back the door and crashed it against Jack a second time. Then he stepped to the side to see Jack teetering with his arms wheeling for balance.

Cassidy didn't let him regain his wits and with desperation fuelling his motion he threw a piledriving blow at Jack's face. It connected with his nose with a satisfying crunch and threw him on his back.

While Jack thrust a hand to his face, the pain removing his willingness to fight back for a moment, Cassidy wrested his gun from his grasp and stood back. By the time Jack had removed his hand and looked up, Cassidy was standing over him with the gun aimed down at his chest.

'It seems as if it'll be you,' he said, 'who'll get a taste of being a prisoner.'

Five minutes later his two guards were locked up in the small room and Cassidy was riding to Monotony.

Full darkness without the benefit of moonlight was approaching fast and the urgency added speed to Cassidy's hurried return. Many hours had passed since Benjamin's departure and only his failure to return gave him hope that the showdown hadn't happened yet.

He approached the town at an angle that let him look down the main road. Few people were outside, an unusual situation in the early evening that helped to increase his anxiety.

Closer, he saw that the people who were outside were congregating by the hotel. Many of them were the men who had captured him and they were watching the saloon. He couldn't see Benjamin with them.

Cassidy headed to the saloon, gathering the men's attention. They looked at him then at each other, clearly surprised to see him being free, but before they could get their wits about them, he dismounted then hurried into the saloon. The moment he'd pushed through the batwings he saw that Walker Matlock was standing beside the door.

The rest of the customers had backed away to the walls and they were doing their best to stay out of whatever trouble was about to erupt. Cassidy breathed a sigh of relief.

'You fine?' he asked.

'I'm taking care of the situation,' Walker said.

'And Millicent?'

'She's safe and out of trouble.'

'There won't be any trouble.' Cassidy looked over the batwings to see Benjamin's men had moved on into the middle of the road where they were spreading out while eyeing the saloon. Benjamin still wasn't amongst them.

'Benjamin Shaw reckons otherwise, but he'll regret taking me on.'

Cassidy gave a significant glance at the men lined up against Walker then at Walker standing on his own.

'I admire your confidence, but you don't stand a chance.'

'You're not stopping me. This showdown has been a year coming.'

Cassidy was minded to ask why he was so determined, but with a shrug he raised his hands slightly and took a backwards step inviting Walker to do as he'd promised.

Walker nodded then glanced over the batwings to appraise the forces aligned against him. Then he moved to push outside, but Cassidy darted in, drawing his gun in a swift motion and slamming it into the small of Walker's back.

'Reach,' he muttered in Walker's ear. 'You're under arrest.'

'You varmint,' Walker said, straightening. 'I should have known you'd side with Benjamin again.'

'I didn't side with Benjamin last year and I'm not doing that now. Last time I let you both go free and that ended in disaster, so this time I'm doing what I should have done back then. I'm arresting you both.'

Cassidy dug his gun in for emphasis and reluctantly Walker raised his hands. Then, with Cassidy keeping the pressure on his back, he had no choice but to step out on to the boardwalk. Cassidy pushed Walker to the side so that Benjamin's men could see the situation then moved him on to the sheriff's office.

'What crime am I supposed to have committed?' Walker said as they walked.

'Two of the town's main citizens are dead. You and Benjamin will stay locked up until I get to the truth.'

Walker firmed his shoulders and took a deep breath suggesting he was about to retort, but he didn't get a chance to speak when Benjamin emerged from the hotel.

'Move aside, Cassidy,' he called out. 'I'll deal with him.'

Cassidy considered Benjamin then the men with him, noting they were standing with their hands dangling beside their holsters waiting for the order to act. The law office was ten paces ahead and judging that waiting until he had help was the best option he continued at a fast walking pace.

Benjamin shouted more taunts at them, but both men ignored him. They reached the door and filed inside.

'Floyd,' Cassidy said, 'we've got trouble.'

Cassidy looked around the office, not seeing the deputy. He gestured for Walker to stand against a wall where he'd be out of view of the men outside, then set about looking for a note from Floyd to explain why he'd left his prisoner against his explicit instructions. But Walker coughed and then pointed at the cells.

At first Cassidy didn't see what had interested him, seeing only the prisoner lying on his cot, but then he saw the problem. Walking sideways to keep Walker in view he headed to the cell to confirm what he thought he'd seen, then gestured for Walker to get the key and free the imprisoned deputy.

Floyd proved to be unconscious and when Walker had dragged him out of the cell it took several slaps to the cheeks to rouse him.

'What. . . ? Who. . . ?' Floyd murmured, still disorientated.

'I'd like to ask you the same questions,' Cassidy said.

143

'I don't know. Millicent came in with a cake and I ate it by the cells.' Floyd winced and rubbed the back of his head. 'Can't remember nothing after that.'

Cassidy helped him to his feet then to a chair.

'Rockwell must have jumped you and escaped.' Cassidy looked up to see that Walker was smiling, making Cassidy snort. 'Don't look pleased. This changes nothing.'

Walker shook his head. 'It changes everything. If Rockwell's free, no matter how many men Benjamin has, it won't be enough.'

Cassidy narrowed his eyes. 'Except you already knew that or you wouldn't have been so confident before. That adds another crime to your list.'

'What list? I came here to find out who killed my mother. I wasn't interested in killing Sheriff Johanson or Judge Mitchell.'

Cassidy glanced through the window. Benjamin and his men had grouped up while looking at the office, obviously discussing what they did next. He turned back to Walker.

'We can start with you playing dead for a year and winding Benjamin up so much he wants to kill you for real.'

'I told you what happened. For months I thought I'd die. Even after I'd fought off the infection I was too weak to protect myself and too poor to keep Rockwell hired. Elizabeth took me in. When I got better, I accepted her plan to get money off Stanley Shaw. If that deal was a crime, I'm not sure what.'

'We both know that's a lie.'

'We don't. Benjamin shot me to hell. You saw that. Did you expect me to shrug it off?'

Cassidy opened his mouth to reply, but then he noticed a crumb of discarded cake on the floor by the cell and a thought he didn't want to entertain tapped at his thoughts.

'Open your shirt,' he said. 'Show me where you got shot to hell.'

With a shrug Walker unbuttoned his shirt, drew up his vest then wriggled until he'd raised it enough to show Cassidy his chest.

'Not pretty, eh?'

Cassidy winced, noting the raised and livid scar tissue that mottled his chest, something Millicent couldn't help but have seen.

'Walker,' he said, 'I have bad news for you.'

CHAPTER 13

Walker Matlock headed out of the law office, his gun at his hip, his face set grimly. He stopped on the boardwalk and faced Benjamin, who gestured to his men to spread out. Then he peeled away from them and faced him.

'It's time we sorted this out,' Walker said.

'I agree,' Benjamin said cautiously, 'but the lawman has other ideas.'

'Not any more.'

Walker glanced over his shoulder at Cassidy as he emerged from the office to stand behind him.

'The way I figure it,' Cassidy said, 'you two will shoot each other up no matter what I do. But if you do it while I'm here, it won't drag anyone else into your quarrel.'

Benjamin considered him then gave a slow nod. He moved backward in a steady arc while keeping Walker and Cassidy in view to stand square-on to the road. He gave a brief gesture to his men that made them also back away to stand on the opposite boardwalk, where they eyed the developing situation with interest.

Walker waited until he was sure they wouldn't attack him then paced out into the road until he was facing Benjamin. Cassidy stayed on the boardwalk outside the sheriff's office.

'I've waited a year to make you pay for my time in jail,' Benjamin said.

'I've waited a year to make you pay for shooting me,' Walker said.

'I didn't.'

'I know that now,' Walker said, making Benjamin narrow his eyes, 'but for the last week I've wanted to make someone pay for killing my mother.'

Walker raised his eyebrows, inviting Benjamin to continue exchanging views.

'That had nothing to do with me either.'

'I know that too because I now know who killed her. So I no longer hate you.'

Benjamin sneered. 'You expect me to believe that?'

Walker moved his hand with extreme slowness to his holster, ensuring that Benjamin saw his every movement. Accordingly, when Walker touched his gun Benjamin followed his action in slowly drawing his own gun, but Walker kept the weapon aimed downwards.

'You will,' Walker said, 'when you see me kill the

man who shot her.'

Walker looked into Benjamin's eyes ensuring he had his full attention. Then he swung his gaze in a slow and deliberate manner to take in the sheriff's office. In a sudden whirl of motion he turned at hip while crouching down, his gun swinging round to the office then moving up to the room above.

Caught in a moment of indecision Benjamin jerked his gun up to aim at Walker then saw that he wasn't planning to shoot him and looked up. From his position beneath the covered boardwalk Cassidy couldn't see what Walker saw there, but by the time he'd stepped out onto the hardpan Walker was peppering lead at an upstairs window.

Glass shattered. A grunt of pain sounded. An ill-directed shot pinged down into the road, kicking dust to Walker's side.

Walker jerked away then took aim again at the window, but he didn't fire when creaking and scuffling feet sounded, suggesting a struggle was underway upstairs.

Cassidy came out into the road looking up and saw Rockwell Trent and Zachary McKinney leaning out of the window with their arms entwined as they both tried to throw the other out. Lurking behind them was Millicent.

Zachary got the upper hand and pushed Rockwell away. Rockwell teetered then fell but he still had a grip of Zachary's arm and both men went tumbling. They hit the boardwalk canopy

148

and rolled towards the edge, but before they could plummet to the ground Benjamin's men got their wits about them.

As one they turned their guns on Walker, who was still watching the fighting twosome.

'Wait!' Benjamin said, raising a hand.

For several long moments everyone stood poised. Then the two men reached the edge of the canopy and fell. They hit the ground heavily on their sides and temporarily stunned they lay slumped.

Walker firmed his gun, seeking to pick off Zachary McKinney while gesturing at Benjamin to join him, but one of Benjamin's men must have interpreting his movement as a hostile one and he loosed off a shot at him. It flew wild but it made Benjamin round on him. He was too late to make his men desist as the shot spurred the rest on to get Walker in their sights.

Lead pinged by him and tore into the ground. Walker swung round aiming to take on his attackers, but he chose discretion when he saw that he faced numerous men and they had all raised their guns.

'This way,' Cassidy shouted from the boardwalk, beckoning him on. He ducked away when a volley of ill-directed shots peppered the office wall behind him.

He looked past Benjamin, who was still waving at his men, but he was doing so half-heartedly as if he was in two minds as to whether or not he should be seeking to stop them.

Cassidy picked out the nearest man, who was following Walker's progress to the boardwalk with a steady hand, but before the man could shoot at Walker, Cassidy tore off a shot. Unerringly, the slug ripped into his upper chest and made him swing away.

This had the unfortunate effect of redirecting everyone's attention to him. Cassidy stood his ground and aimed at a second man, but when his shot flew wide he decided to join Walker in fleeing to safety. He turned and ran with slugs kicking at his heels.

Another volley tore splinters from the door jamb and then Cassidy bounded through the open doorway. His momentum kept him running on for several paces before he managed to slide to a halt and turn.

He moved back to the door to cover Walker on his way in, but Walker had already dived to the boardwalk and as stray bullets whined through the open doorway he slid on his belly to safety.

The two men nodded to each other. Then they scrambled to their feet and they each took a window on either side of the door.

'Where's Floyd?' Walker asked.

Cassidy looked around the office, but he failed to see him.

'He was groggy. But hopefully he's somewhere

where he can help us.'

Cassidy peered out to see that Benjamin and his men were scurrying into covered positions behind barrels and into alleys.

Rockwell and Zachary were still wrestling on the ground beside the boardwalk. Each man was trying to pin the other down, but the shock of their tumble had weakened them and neither man was being effective in his attempt to subdue the other.

'You reckon Benjamin's in control of his guns?' Cassidy asked.

'No,' Walker said, watching Benjamin disappear from view across the road. 'That's the trouble when you get involved with men like them.'

Cassidy cast a significant glance at Rockwell and Zachary.

'Sure,' he said.

A further comment was on his lips but he didn't get to utter it when the men across the road got themselves organized and a frenzied volley of slugs tore through the windows.

Glass shards flew making Cassidy duck away as lead ricocheted around the law office. He kept his head down, choosing his moment to return fire, but then he heard footfalls pounding across the boardwalk.

He bobbed up to see Rockwell Trent beating a retreat to the office while Zachary McKinney lay in the road on his back winded. Cassidy had never expected to see Rockwell running from trouble, but then again Rockwell had been only a shadow of his formidable reputation.

On the run Rockwell reached the doorway. A gunshot rang out. Rockwell threw his arms up, his back arching, a muttered oath of pain on his lips. He staggered on for a pace through the door, then pitched over to land on his chest.

Smoke rose from a hole in his back and when Cassidy looked through the broken window he saw that Zachary McKinney had hit him while retreating. Cassidy loosed off a shot at him but it clattered wide as he disappeared from view to his left.

Walker shouted at Cassidy to cover him. Then he risked moving into a position where he could be seen through the doorway. He dragged Rockwell to the side. He leant over him, frowned then looked up at Cassidy and shook his head.

'He won't be helping us,' he said.

'Pity,' Cassidy said. 'Despite everything we could have done with having him on our side.'

Walker rocked back on his haunches, still shaking his head.

'I never thought I'd see the Iceman killed so easily.'

'From what I saw his reputation was greater than the man.'

Walker frowned as he returned to his window. He took in the scene outside confirming that nobody was in view.

'Something changed him. He wasn't the same

man I first used.'

'Why did you hire him the first time?'

'I'd heard rumours someone was planning to kill me. It was making me edgy and so when Benjamin confronted me I thought it was him. . . .' Walker sighed. 'I'd never have believed it was my own wife who'd hired Zachary McKinney to kill me.'

Cassidy considered the various positions that Benjamin's men had taken up.

'Let's hope that now Benjamin knows you don't blame him it'll be enough for him to call off his men.'

Walker sneered. 'That won't happen. You've still got it into your head that he's the decent man and I'm the aggressor. You were wrong last year and you're wrong now.'

Cassidy couldn't think of an answer to that, but he decided the better response was to prove he was right.

'Hey, Benjamin,' he shouted. 'Blood's been shed and men have died, but that doesn't mean more men have to die over a feud that nobody needs to continue.'

He waited for an answer, seeing several men edge into view as they waited to hear Benjamin's response.

'This has already gone too far,' Benjamin said finally, his tone sounding resigned. 'Nothing will take away my year in prison.'

'Nothing will, but Walker now knows who shot him and it wasn't you. The man you have a problem with isn't Walker; it's Zachary McKinney. Let's join together and get him.'

Cassidy ducked down while he awaited an answer, and from the muttered words he heard from across the road clearly his comment was being considered. Then he got his answer.

A sustained burst of gunfire tore out. Cassidy flinched, preparing himself for a shower of glass cascading down from the remaining panes, but it didn't come.

'Some of them have taken up your offer,' Walker said from the other window.

Cassidy grunted a snort of approval then bobbed up to see that three of Benjamin's men had swung into view and they were firing to the side of the sheriff's office, presumably at Zachary.

Returning gunfire tore along the side of the hotel and one man stood up straight then keeled over as Zachary found a target. This made most of the remaining men duck out of view, but Benjamin moved into a prominent position facing the sheriff's office. He swung his gun up and fired.

Lead flew through the window and pinged off a cell bar at the far end of the office.

'I said we couldn't trust Benjamin,' Walker complained then tore off a shot at him.

Cassidy stayed his fire as he appraised the situation, but when Benjamin again fired, this time

154

sending a slug into the side of the window and spraying splinters down on him, he joined Walker.

They both laid down sustained gunfire that forced Benjamin to dive for cover. Walker grunted with approval while Cassidy sat back down with his back to the wall to reload.

'I'm surprised he turned on us,' Cassidy said.

'I'm not,' Walker muttered as he joined Cassidy in reloading.

Cassidy was punching in the first slug when the thought came that perhaps Benjamin had also been trying to shoot Zachary. He jerked his head towards the door a moment before Zachary dived through, his leap to safety being accompanied by several slugs that ripped into the door frame.

Zachary rolled over a shoulder and came up on one knee in a position where he couldn't be seen from outside, but he did have both Walker and Cassidy in view. He turned his gun on Walker while glaring at Cassidy, but when he saw that these were the only two men left inside, he smiled.

'Obliged you kept Benjamin pinned down,' he said.

'But not any more,' Cassidy said. 'He won't give up now he knows who's responsible.'

'Do you really think that'll concern the man who killed Rockwell Trent?'

'Rockwell wasn't the man he once was.'

'He wasn't, but then again, who do you think took him down one piece at a time?' Zachary

155

waited for an answer that Cassidy wasn't prepared to offer. Then he swung his gun round to aim at Cassidy. 'But in yours and Walker's case, I won't delay the inevitable.'

Zachary's eyes narrowed with a hint that he was about to fire. Armed with only an unloaded gun Cassidy had no choice but to throw the weapon at him, but before he launched it, a gunshot tore out.

Cassidy winced, expecting pain, but nothing came. A six-shooter clattered off Zachary's shoulder as Walker carried out the same action as he had been about to enact. Then Zachary stumbled but it wasn't because of the well-aimed missile.

Behind him and forgotten about, Rockwell had been playing dead. He'd raised his gun to sight Zachary's back.

With a stumbling gait Zachary turned to face him and for a moment the two adversaries locked gazes. Then a second shot ripped out and sliced straight between Zachary's eyes.

Zachary keeled over.

Rockwell watched him approvingly then nodded to himself. He moved to holster his gun, but the weapon fell from his fingers. He considered the weapon lying at his side then looked up at Cassidy.

'He should have finished the job,' he said.

He rolled on to his back and exhaled a long breath then stilled. This time Cassidy was sure he wasn't pretending.

He got to his feet aiming to let Benjamin know

that the situation was now under control, but Walker cast him a concerned look.

'It's over,' Cassidy said.

'But not for me,' Walker said. 'Zachary said he was responsible for what happened to Benjamin, except he wasn't.'

Cassidy furrowed his brow, but then he realized what Walker had meant.

'Millicent,' he said.

CHAPTER 14

Cassidy stood to the side of the door. While coming up the stairs people had been talking inside but now they had quietened.

As far as he could tell Millicent had come up to the old storeroom above the law office with Rockwell and Zachary. He hoped she was still here as tracking her down would be hard on everyone.

He backhanded the door open then coughed before he spoke up, but he found out that he hadn't needed to warn her.

'The situation's under control, Cassidy,' Deputy Wright said.

Cassidy swung into the doorway. Floyd was holding Millicent beside the window. She had lowered her head showing she wouldn't give them any trouble. Cassidy took no chances and kept his gun on her.

'You're under arrest,' he said.

This comment made her look up and provide a cold smile.

'Why?'

'For the record, last year you hired Zachary McKinney to kill Walker Matlock, and then later to kill the rest of the Matlock family, presumably for their wealth.'

She shrugged as if this matter didn't concern her.

'I heard some of what was said down there. Zachary's dead. You'll never prove I hired him.'

Cassidy fixed her with his harsh gaze. She might be right, but her cold tone that was so unlike her usual speaking voice convinced him that her appealing exterior masked a heartless individual.

'Sadly for you Zachary told me everything before he died.'

Before she could respond he beckoned Floyd to take her to the sheriff's office. As the deputy dragged her away, this time screeching and struggling, Cassidy hurried on ahead to the road and to his concern he found that the other confrontation he'd expected was taking place.

In the centre of the road Benjamin and Walker were facing each other. Cassidy moved into a position where they would see him, but his concern was misplaced.

'The last year was tough on you,' Walker said using a calm and understanding voice.

'It was bad for you too,' Benjamin said, matching Walker's tone.

Walker nodded. Then, with that being the

extent of the forgiving either man was prepared to do today, they turned away. Benjamin headed across the road to the hotel where his father emerged to welcome him.

There'd be no such warm welcome for Walker though as when he turned it was to see that Floyd was escorting the still struggling and complaining Millicent to the law office.

He caught her eye with a narrowed-eyed glare that made her look away. Then he came over to join Cassidy.

'This is over,' he said.

'I'm glad to hear it,' Cassidy said. 'But don't be downhearted. It was better to know the truth than to continue to live a lie.'

'I guess.'

'And like Benjamin, your father's still waiting for you to return to him properly. You should go and sit with him.'

'I'll do that.' Walker moved to head down the road. He stopped and looked back. 'But if you've finished here, you could come and sit with him too. I gather there were things he wanted to tell you.'

Cassidy joined him and offered a smile.

'And now is the right time for me to hear them,' he said.